TEN

Andrej Longo

TEN

Translated from the Italian by
Howard Curtis

HARVILL SECKER
LONDON

Published by Harvill Secker 2013

2 4 6 8 10 9 7 5 3 1

First published with the title *Dieci* in 2007
by Adelphi Edizioni, Milan

First published in Great Britain in 2013 by
HARVILL SECKER
Random House
20 Vauxhall Bridge Road
London SW1V 2SA

www.vintage-books.co.uk

Addresses for companies within The Random House Group Limited
can be found at: www.randomhouse.co.uk/offices.htm

The Random House Group Limited Reg. No. 954009

A CIP catalogue record for this book is available from the British Library

ISBN 9781846556173 (trade paperback)
ISBN 9781448105779 (ebook)

The Random House Group Limited supports The Forest Stewardship Council® (FSC®), the leading international forest-certification organisation. Our books carrying the FSC label are printed on FSC®-certified paper. FSC is the only forest-certification scheme supported by the leading environmental organisations, including Greenpeace. Our paper procurement policy can be found at www.randomhouse.co.uk/environment

Typeset in Aldus Lt Std and Palatino by
Palimpsest Book Production Ltd, Falkirk, Stirlingshire
Printed and bound CPI Group (UK) Ltd, Croydon, CR0 4YY

To the lovely Lucy

I

I AM THE LORD THY GOD, THOU SHALT HAVE NO OTHER GODS BEFORE ME

Vanessa's well fit. When she puts on those black stockings and that short leather skirt, you'd think she was a grown woman. When she gets her eyeliner on and goes out in those heels, she can really make your head spin, even though she's only fourteen, even though she laughs like a little girl.

'Vanè,' I always say to her, 'you're gorgeous.'

'Are you jealous or something?' she answers.

Of course I'm jealous. It's only natural. But that's not the point. The point is, she likes to show off what she's got, she gets more gorgeous every day, and sooner or later something's going to happen, I know it is, but I don't say anything because I don't want it to be too obvious that I'm worried.

* * *

Watch out, Papilù. Don't cause trouble, Papilù. Listen to me, Papilù, don't interfere. Nobody's forcing you, Papilù, you're a good lad. For Christ's sake, Papilù.

For the times we live in, I feel like a responsible guy. I've made up my mind I don't want to end up like my dad, always in and out of prison.

I study, and in the afternoons I work in a bar, serving coffee, trying to stay out of everyone's way, especially Giggino Mezzanotte's people. Giggino Mezzanotte runs things around here, and they call him Mezzanotte because he's more of a night person. They all suck up to him, like he's a god or something, because they all want a piece of the cake. Some people want to deal, some want to hide drugs and guns, or sell fakes, or get a job on a building site or in a cleaning business. But I don't want anything from Giggino Mezzanotte, not now, not ever, because once you're inside the system you're fucked and your life's not your own any more. He decides everything for you, he tells you what to do and what not to do, and if you don't stick to the rules you can bet he'll put a bullet in your head. Because that's how things work around here. They give you a few scraps every now and again, to keep you sweet, to trick you into thinking that sooner or later you'll be doing all right. In the meantime they're putting away millions in the bank, buying speedboats and fancy cars, building high-security villas, they make sure they do all right out of it, that's the way they are, just like politicians, who come out with all those fine words and then just take advantage. They're even worse, all they think about is votes and how to get more of them. And every now and again, when the bodies start piling up and the newspapers kick up a stink, they send the police in to make a few arrests, to throw smoke in people's eyes, to make themselves look good on TV, to make it look like they're concerned. But they don't really care. They don't give a fuck. To them we're the scum of the world. That's what we are. Scum.

But when you're seventeen you can't just carry on serving coffee and pretending everything's fine, because then you end up serving coffee all your life. And life isn't going to wait for you like they wait for their coffee. I mean, don't hold your breath for something to happen. And you don't know what to do, you don't know where to start. You try to keep out of trouble, to study, but you know you won't find work afterwards anyway, not here. Let's say for example I want to be a mechanic and open my own repair shop. Let's say I actually find the money to open it. What happens after I've opened it? Somebody comes along and says, 'Papilù, if you want everything to carry on nice and quiet, you have to give me so much a month.'

Guaranteed.

So then you decide to give them what they ask you, because you want to live a quiet life and stay out of trouble, you know it's not right but you give them so much a month.

But it's not enough, it's never enough. They're like rats. First they're shut up inside the house and then they're lounging in the sun because they're not scared of anything. They're just like rats, the more they eat the hungrier they get because they've got a taste for it. So you know that after a while they're going to come asking for more.

And then what do you do? Call the police? To say what?

'Excuse me, I have rats and now they're lounging about, can you come and clean my house up?'

If you call the police, it's all over. They'll shoot you in the legs one day when you're on your way home, and then burn down your shop. That's why you can't open a shop. So tell me what you can do. That's right, what can you do? You're young. Your hormones are working like crazy. You've got energy bursting out of your skin. You can't wait. You can't keep pretending everything's OK.

Watch out, Papilù. Don't cause trouble, Papilù. Listen to me, Papilù, don't interfere. Nobody's forcing you, Papilù, you're a good lad. For Christ's sake, Papilù.

* * *

Before I went downstairs I did twenty press-ups, first with the right arm, then with the left. Then I gelled my hair back and put my knife in the pocket of my jeans and my dog tag around my neck, because everyone round here wears a dog tag, with their name and date of birth and blood group on it. On the back of mine, I had them put Vanessa's name.

As I was on my way out my mum said, 'Don't come back too late, Papilù.'

I didn't answer her. I feel sorry for my mum. She's young, she's still a good-looking woman, and she has to live like a nun because that's the rule. Because that's what Giggino Mezzanotte and people like him have decided. And that's what you have to do.

I went out, started up my moped and went to pick up Vanessa.

Vanessa looks fucking amazing tonight. Proper done up, with her blonde hair smelling of apples and that Vaniti perfume that'd turn me on even if I was blind.

She kisses me on the mouth.

'Vanè, you're gorgeous.'

'All right, don't go getting all jealous on me.'

She gets on the moped and grabs onto me, and we head off.

It's Saturday. We usually go out on Fridays, because it's quieter and there's never any trouble. We go to a pub or a club that plays hip hop. You're safe on Friday. No trouble. Normal people who just want to enjoy themselves. But she wants to go out on Saturday. I understand her. All her friends go out on Saturday. Saturday is something else. Everyone's out and about, you start to feel the adrenalin kick out on the streets, and in the clubs everyone's off their fucking faces before they even get started. That's why you never know who you're going to meet or what might happen. I managed to make excuses at first, but I could sense she was going off me. So tonight we're going over towards Pozzuoli to hear some house.

The club is still half empty. The people who are there seem OK. It's mostly couples. Couples don't cause trouble. There's even a group of girls on their own. And three or four guys who are pissing about to get some attention. I feel more relaxed. We start dancing.

Why talk when you can dance?
Dance and don't stop,
Don't talk, just take a chance,
Dance till you drop.

'Fancy a drink, Vanè?'
'What?'
'How about a drink?'
'I can't hear you.'

'Do you want a drink?'

'Later. Let's dance.'

Vanessa laughs. She dances. She laughs. She's like a gazelle in those heels. Squeezed into that leather skirt and that cotton top. Like the filling inside a plate of cannelloni. Like a peach you want to bite into. She laughs. She knows I can't take my eyes off her. She laughs. She dances faster.

'Vanè, you're amazing.'

'What?'

'You're amazing.'

'What did you say?'

'You're really gorgeous.'

She laughs and keeps dancing.

The lights go on and off. Light. Dark. Light. Dark. Vanessa's eyes light up. They close. They light up again. Light. Dark. Light. Dark. She spins round twice, like a top. Her hair is like a blue wave. Red. Green. Blue again.

Why think when you can dance?
Have fun, don't stop,
Don't think, just take a chance,
Dance till you drop.

'Papilù, I'm thirsty.'

'What?'

'I'm thirsty.'

'What did you say?'

'I want a drink.'

'OK, let's have a drink.'

We move through the crowd to the bar. By now, the club is almost full. The music comes thudding out of the loud-speakers. You can feel it deep inside you, it almost hurts.

'Come on, everybody, dance!' the DJ screams, turning up the volume. The lights go on and off again.

Why eat when you can dance?
Get out there, don't stop,
Don't eat, just take a chance,
Dance till you drop.

'What do you want?'

'A Coke.'

'Do you want a bit of whisky in it?'

'OK, why not?'

'Two whisky and Cokes please.'

She's standing next to the bar. She's bathed in sweat and her top is half soaked and clinging to her. I kiss her on her ear. She laughs and throws her head back. I kiss her on the neck. Then on the mouth. Tongue to tongue.

'Wow, you're on it tonight.'

'You're killing me, Vanè!'

She laughs and drinks a bit of her whisky and Coke and sways slowly in time to the music.

Why talk when you can dance?
Dance and don't stop,
Don't talk, just take a chance,
Dance till you drop.

'Want a cigarette?'
She nods.
We go outside with our glasses.
We smoke.
'Saturday's something else,' she says.
'Do you like it?'
She nods.
I kiss her again.
We smoke.
I glance at my watch.
'It's nearly midnight,' I say.
'Let's dance some more,' she says.
'Won't your mum say anything?'
She shrugs and throws the cigarette on the ground. We finish the whisky and Cokes and go back inside.

Why think when you can dance?
Have fun, don't stop,

Don't think, just take a chance,
Dance till you drop.

The place is crammed. There's hardly any space on the dance floor. As we're trying to squeeze through, somebody bashes into me with his shoulder. Hard. I look at him. He's wearing mirrored sunglasses and a cap on backwards.

'Did I hurt you?' he says.

'No, no,' I say.

'Your girlfriend has a nice arse,' he says.

I look at him for a moment.

Watch out, Papilù. Don't cause trouble, Papilù. Listen to me, Papilù, don't interfere. Nobody's forcing you, Papilù, you're a good lad.

'I know,' I answer him.

I catch up with Vanessa, who's already dancing.

I start dancing with her.

Why eat when you can dance?
Get out there, don't stop,
Don't eat, just take a chance,
Dance till you drop.

'What did he want?'

'Who?'

'Him.'

'Who?'
'The guy with the dark glasses.'
'Oh. Nothing.'

Why talk when you can dance?
Dance and don't stop,
Don't talk, just take a chance,
Dance till you drop.

'I'm a bit dizzy,' she says.
'Do you feel sick?'
She shakes her head. She stops for a moment.
'I'm dizzy,' she says.
She laughs and slips a hand inside my T-shirt.
'Do you love me?' she asks.
'A lot.'
Another laugh. She starts dancing again.

Why think when you can dance?
Have fun, don't stop,
Don't think, just take a chance,
Dance till you drop.

'There he is,' Vanessa says.
'What?'
'There he is.'
'Who?

She makes a sign with her head, pointing behind me.

I turn. The guy with the dark glasses is dancing very near us. He's looking at me and smiling like he's taking the piss. He does a turn, clapping his hands two or three times. Then he bends his knees and goes down until he's close to the floor. He moves his tongue over his lips. It's like he's possessed or something. His dog tag goes up and down on his chest as he dances.

'Let's get out of here,' I say.

'What?'

'Let's get out of here.'

'Why?'

'Just move.'

I grab her by the arm and take her with me. The exit seems like it's a long time coming.

Why eat when you can dance?
Get out there, don't stop,
Don't eat, just take a chance,
Dance till you drop.

At last we're outside, in the middle of the street.

'What's the matter?' she says.

'It's late.'

'Are you kidding?'

'I'll get the moped and we'll go,' I say.

I haven't gone far when the door of the club opens

and the guy with the mirrored glasses comes out. He has two other guys with him. They also have their caps on backwards.

'Going already?' he says to Vanessa.

'What's it to you?' she replies.

He laughs. The other two also laugh.

I stand closer to Vanessa.

He puts his hand inside his jacket. I put my hand on my knife. He takes a packet of cigarettes from his jacket pocket. He smiles again. In the dark I can see his earring shining.

'Cigarette?'

'I don't smoke,' Vanessa replies.

He puts a cigarette in his mouth. He lowers his glasses a bit to look at her.

'Why don't you send your friend home to bed and stay here with us?'

From inside the disco we can hear the music booming away.

> *Why talk when you can dance?*
> *Dance and don't stop,*
> *Don't talk, just take a chance,*
> *Dance till you drop.*

It's now or never, I think. If I do it now I might still get away with it. If I drag it out too long I'm fucked.

'Why don't you go back inside with your friends and dance?' I say.

He looks surprised. He wasn't expecting that. He didn't think I had it in me.

He opens and closes his eyes two or three times.

'I'm sorry, what did you say?'

I can see the reflection of the club sign in his dark glasses.

Why think when you can dance?
Have fun, don't stop,
Don't think, just take a chance,
Dance till you drop.

I take Vanessa by the hand and pull her away.

'Where are you going?' the guy in the glasses says.

He takes a step towards us.

I take out my knife. 'Home to bed.'

He moves his tongue over his lips. It's obvious he's off his face on something.

'You shouldn't have done that,' he says.

A knife appears in his hand. And the two others also have knives in their hands. Vanessa hides behind me.

She starts shaking.

'How about you leave us the girl and go and we won't do anything to you?' he says.

'Fuck off,' I say.

'I didn't quite hear that,' he says.
'Fuck off,' I repeat.

Why eat when you can dance?
Get out there, don't stop,
Don't eat, just take a chance,
Dance till you drop.

I look right and left. I see the other two moving to surround me. Vanessa is clinging to me even harder. The guy with glasses is ready to strike. I've got myself in the shit, I think. Things are going to end really badly this time.

'So, what do you want to do?' he says.

If I get him first, I may still get away with it. Maybe his friends would just stand there and let me go. It won't be easy but I don't have any alternative. With my arm, I move Vanessa back a bit. I tighten my grip on the knife. My hand is hurting.

Why talk when you can dance?
Dance and don't stop,
Don't talk, just take a chance,
Dance till you drop.

'Hey, Papilù, what are you doing here?' says a voice. The voice comes from out of the darkness. For a while nobody moves. We stand there with our knives in our hands and the blood throbbing in our muscles and the music still pumping away.

Why think when you can dance?
Have fun, don't stop,
Don't think, just take a chance,
Dance till you drop.

'Anything wrong, Papilù?' says the voice.

And from out of the dark comes Giggino Mezzanotte. All dressed up and smiling away. With his polished shoes and his jacket thrown over his arm. Along with two half-naked women, and bodyguards like mountains.

He puts his hand on my elbow, calm as anything.

'Everything OK, son?' he says.

The guy with the mirrored glasses puts his knife in his pocket. His two friends do the same. Without a word they go back inside the club.

'Yes,' I say. 'Yes, everything's fine.'

'Good,' he says.

He slaps me on the shoulder.

As he walks back towards the entrance to the club, he says, 'You and me must have a chat one of these days.'

'All right,' I say.

He turns and looks at me.

'Come and see me tomorrow at eleven. You know where to find me, don't you?'

'Yes,' I say, 'I know.'

'I'll expect you tomorrow,' he says.

2

THOU SHALT NOT TAKE THE NAME OF THE LORD THY GOD IN VAIN

I used to have dark, smouldering eyes and a tenor voice, and when I sang people got cold shivers even if it was forty degrees. At first I sang in church, during Mass, or else at christenings, and at Christmas and Easter. They used to say I was an angel sent from heaven, nobody in the neighbourhood had ever heard a voice like that before, with that voice I had to be an angel of God.

At eighteen I started singing at parties thrown by powerful people. They competed over me. Weddings, confirmations, birthdays, everybody wanted Saverio; they were all after me, and they paid me in hundred-euro notes, they gave me champagne and rum baba and all the rest, they invited me to their summer villas and on their yachts, they invited me everywhere, and I always went, I never said no, I never let anyone down, and when I started to sing they were all blown away.

It's your eyes
that made me fall in love,
it's your eyes
that won't let me sleep.

I used to be as handsome as a god, I'd take girls down into the cellar of my dad's pastry shop and fuck them on the table where my father made his pastries.

'No, Savè, no, what are you doing?' they'd all say.

They'd lie down on the table and make a fuss when I parted their thighs.

'No, Savè, no, what are you doing?'

But they'd stay, because of those smouldering eyes, and that tenor voice that no woman could resist.

I used to have good muscles, I was as strong as a bull, I could sing twenty hours a day, in the heat and the cold, I never got tired, I could fuck all night, I never let up. I could conquer the world, I thought, and nobody could stop me.

I used to go around on a motorbike, in my silk jacket and designer shoes, with the wind blowing in my hair and a handkerchief round my neck, like a film star. And the women who watched me go by all dreamt that I'd dedicate a song to them, they'd have paid just for an hour in my dad's cellar, lying on the table where he kneaded the dough.

I used to play cards without my hand shaking, I could make a bundle even if I only had two kings because I looked confident and kept my breathing steady and didn't know what fear was. The number of men I ruined on those winter nights, the number I saw swallowed up by life, and I'd think, Not me, life will never swallow me up, not in a million years.

I used to imagine that when I was tired of doing what I was doing I'd buy a house in the country, with a fireplace and a terrace with an arbour, I'd raise buffaloes to make mozzarella, and I'd find a nice cheerful girl who'd give me six or seven kids. The kids would play in the orchard, and I'd sit in my armchair smoking a Havana cigar, and from the kitchen the smell of pasta and beans, or macaroni, would waft out. And every now and again I'd bake something for the kids, a fruit tart, for instance – I was always good at baking those, there weren't many around who could bake them as well as me.

That's what I used to think about, that and other things, not even all that long ago, let's say five years, maybe six, so that now, looking at myself in the mirror, I say to myself, Savè, what the hell happened to you?

Then I try not to think about it, to look somewhere else, at my shoes, my hands, and sometimes I stand in front of the mirror like that for a whole hour, not wanting to do anything, not making up my mind to get dressed and start another day. I'd like to find the man who reduced me to this state and pick a fight with him, I'd like to shoot him, and maybe then I'd get this weight off my shoulders and feel lighter.

I'd like to find him, but there isn't anyone. And there isn't anyone because the fault is all mine.

So I get dressed and try to get through another day, hoping it'll be my last, hoping God will have mercy on me and put an end to this whole crazy mess, hoping I won't have to live through another morning.

And yet I had everything I needed to get my slice of the cake. With this voice and these eyes I really could have become someone, it wouldn't have been that hard. All I had to do was take it one step at a time, be a bit more patient. Maybe that's what I lacked, patience. I was in too much of a hurry, as if life was going to slip through my fingers. It's like if someone has an appointment with the Queen and he gets himself all dressed up and scented, and then, for fear he'll arrive late, for fear the Queen will slip through his fingers, he takes the stairs four at a time, trips over, and goes flying downstairs, bangs his head, and that's the last thing he remembers.

I had such a beautiful voice, they even asked for me at funerals. When I sang, people actually forgot the dead for a while.

'Savè, come if you can,' they'd say.

And I'd go, I didn't spare myself.

But after a while, singing at parties and weddings wasn't enough for me. I wasn't content making eight or nine thousand euros a month. I wanted more. I thought because I had that special voice I was immortal – if I wanted I could have cheated death with one verse, I could even have sung God a song and He'd have done anything I asked Him.

I wanted more. I didn't want to wait.

So one evening, at a party with fireworks and the garden all lit up, after all the applause and the handshakes I went to the owner of the villa, who was ordering his people about, and told him about this itch I had, this wanting to go further.

'Maybe you could give me a hand,' I said.

'No problem, Savè.'

He took a sip of champagne.

'I can get you on television, how about that?'

That was all I was looking for. Television. It was my dream.

OK, so it wasn't RAI or even Channel 5 or Sky, it was only local, but it put my name about and I started to get recognised on the street, even outside my own neighbourhood. I was asked for my autograph, and I'd sign, feeling really proud of myself. I thought it was only the beginning, in a year or two I'd be really famous, nobody could stop me now.

I didn't understand anything in those days. It was like I had a fog in my head and saw only what I wanted to see, the only thing I heard was my own voice, the voice of an angel sent from heaven.

So gradually the itch comes back, the impatience. And at his daughter's confirmation party I go again to the owner of the villa.

'Maybe you could give me a hand,' I say.

'No problem, Savè.' He drinks his usual glass of champagne and says, 'I'll arrange for you to make a record, how about that?'

A record sounded good to me.

So there I was, in a recording studio, with headphones on my head, the centre of attention. They even brought in an orchestra to back me up. With the orchestra and the technicians and a journalist writing something in the papers to launch the record, I felt as important as a god. I thought I could do what I wanted and nothing would happen to me. I thought the world was hanging on my every breath, that whether or not the earth kept turning depended on my voice.

The record did well. I was invited everywhere. I went on national radio, I toured, I slept in five-star hotels, and I fucked whoever I wanted. Dancers with long legs they wrapped round me like snakes, TV presenters' assistants with arses as firm as drums, I'd spend the night fucking and the next day singing. There were articles in newspapers and magazines, I even got in the charts.

Another party. I'm already thinking what else I could ask the owner of the villa. This time, though, he's the one who takes me by the arm and leads me out on the terrace.

'Savè,' he says, 'when you wanted me to help you I did.'

'Yes, you did,' I say.

'Now I'd like you to do something for me.'

I didn't miss a beat. I'm not an idiot, I knew he'd ask me for something in return. In fact, I'd been surprised he hadn't asked for anything before.

'What do I have to do?' I ask calmly.

'Nothing big,' he says. 'Just deliver a package to someone on your next tour.'

'No problem.'

We both laugh, and toast each other with champagne, and then I sing for the guests.

On the next tour I deliver the package like I've been told. I'm a bit nervous, obviously, but everything goes well, without a hitch. Just like drinking a glass of water. Just like singing a song.

For a few months nothing happens. Life seems to be gliding calmly by. I feel like I have everything I ever wanted, like there's nothing more I could wish for. But after a while the itch comes back. I have a new obsession. The Sanremo Song Festival. That's the only thing missing. If I can sing there, it'd be a real step up. No one could stop me then. Saverio would be out of sight.

I told the owner of the villa, 'I want to go to Sanremo.'

This time he didn't answer straight away. He looked at the other buildings from his terrace and turned the glass round in his hands, lost in thought.

'Savè,' he said, 'I think for now it's best if you make do with what you've got.'

I realised he couldn't do it. Powerful as he was, with half the city in his pocket, even he couldn't go that far.

But I didn't give up on the idea of Sanremo. If I could find someone more powerful, I thought, I'd get there. There were so many of them, you just needed one with the right connections.

Of course, I had to be careful, I needed to take things slowly, at least at first, at least until I got to Sanremo. So I kept going to parties. If they asked me for a song I never said no, I always ate the rum baba, but in the meantime I was looking around, waiting for the right opportunity.

The opportunity came at the end of summer. I'd gone to the coast to chill out for a few days. I was in a bar, and the pianist there knew me.

'Hey, Savè, what are you doing here?' he said.

So we had a bit of a chat over a Martini, and I ended up by the piano with the microphone in my hand. As I'm not the kind of person who needs to be asked twice, they got my voice and nothing but for the next half an hour.

It's your eyes
that made me fall in love,
it's your eyes
that won't let me sleep.

Afterwards, of course, there were congratulations and handshakes, and autographs for whoever asked for one. And then there was this woman, who couldn't have been far off sixty. It was obvious she was horny, she kept rubbing her thigh against mine while she talked. She wouldn't leave me alone and I didn't know how to get rid of her. I wasn't even listening to her, I was looking for an excuse to leave, but after a while she tells me her husband's a politician. I start to pay more attention to her then, give her a bit of rope, and when I realise she might be the right person to get me to Sanremo, I actually invite her to dance.

An hour later we're in the toilets. Her with her back right up against the wall, wearing nothing but her high-heeled shoes, and me with my hands under her thighs to hold her up and fucking her like there's no tomorrow.

'That's it, don't stop, carry on, that's it.'

She's moaning and whimpering like an alley cat.

'Don't stop, that's it, don't stop.'

To cut a long story short, it turns out this woman could well be the one to get me to Sanremo. Obviously, it's going to take time, but she knows what she's about, she sets up appointments for me with all these people, and everyone says, no problem, they'll get me into the festival for sure. In the meantime I've stopped going to parties and weddings. I find excuses, make up prior engagements, a cold, a business trip. I fuck this woman and think about Sanremo. I can already see myself there, up on the stage, singing in my tenor voice. I fuck the woman and think I've made it. I fuck the woman and imagine that even the Pope would send for me.

Now that time has passed, now that I turn my head away if I see myself in a mirror and don't care about anything any more and am just waiting to die, if ever I have a lucid moment and think about the way I was in those days, I realise what a fucking idiot I was. But I didn't realise it at the time, I thought I'd become like a god, I thought I just had to snap my fingers and I'd have whatever I wanted.

Two months before Sanremo, the woman made herself scarce. I tried to get in touch with her, but she didn't seem to want to know me, apparently just hearing my name turned her stomach. After a while she changed her mobile number.

I realised I could forget about Sanremo.

I got depressed, which is only normal. Anyone would understand it. To get over it I'd snort a bit of coke every now and again, maybe a couple of times a week. I'd done it before, but then it was a social thing, joining in the fun at parties, just so I didn't look like someone who got upset at the sight of a line of coke. Or else sometimes I'd do it when I was worn out after too much work, or if I was going to spend all night fucking. It had happened, but I was fine, I could take it or leave it. But now it was different, now I was sick and it made me feel better.

Gradually, I got over it. I decided I'd go back to singing at parties and weddings. Not to mention the tours, the recordings, the TV appearances. When you came down to it, it wasn't a bad life, I could have been happy with it. True, nobody had called me for a few months, I'd offended them, I realised that, but if I apologised I was sure everything would go back to being the way it was before.

I went back to the villa.

'Savè, you have to be patient,' the man said. 'We've got another singer now. He's not as good as you, but he's a friend. Maybe in a while, we'll see.'

He didn't offer me any champagne. Or even rum baba.

I thought they were just playing with me, keeping me

dangling for a while. All I had to do was hold out for a few months, I thought, they couldn't do without my voice.

In the meantime, there was still local TV and radio, and I'd arrange a few tours.

But after a couple of appearances, the TV channel told me they didn't have authorisation to give me work, and the radio station said I wasn't fashionable any more. As for tours, I did one and got paid expenses only.

Suddenly it was like it was all over, it was like nobody remembered me.

I started to feel a bit scared.

To get over that, I began snorting coke more often. First every other day. Then every day. I always thought I could stop whenever I liked; first I'd sort things out and then I'd stop. In the meantime the money was running out and I didn't know what to do. I still did a few local parties and weddings, where I could find them, but it was piddling stuff, barbecues in gardens with sour wine and a bit of backgammon after dinner.

Maybe at that point it wasn't too late for me to save myself. Maybe I could have gone back to making pastries with my father, because I wasn't too bad at that, my fruit tarts were particularly good. Maybe I could still have found a nice girl and started a family like anyone else. Sure, I'd have a mortgage to pay and never enough money, no cigars, no garden, but at least it would have been something. Compared with what I have now it would have been a fairy tale.

I got depressed and really got into coke in a big way.

I also got into debt. Five or six hundred euros, no more than that.

'Savè,' the owner of the villa said, 'I'd like to help you.'

And he suggested I take coke to some of the local parties I went to.

It isn't so bad, I thought, a temporary situation, everything's going to work out now, I've been through tough times but now my luck's starting to change. I didn't realise I was going downhill. Life was swallowing me up and I didn't even notice. A bit at a time, at first. Then faster and faster.

My voice was all shot because of the coke, it had turned shrill. My eyes weren't as clear as they used to be, they didn't smoulder the way they did before. To keep leading the life I was leading, to keep snorting three times a day, I started making longer journeys, all the way up north. Once a month at first, then every two weeks, then every week. I was working for them now, but I still thought I could get out of it, I still thought the wind would change sooner or later. But the wind never changed, it was blowing in my face so that I couldn't see where I was going, couldn't see I was going downhill. In the meantime I kept snorting, it was like the only way I could get a moment's peace was when I was snorting.

'Savè,' the owner of the villa said to me one evening, 'you're six thousand euros short.'

I asked him to give me a bit of time. I'd soon start singing again, I told him, I already had a contract, in a month I'd sort everything out. For old times' sake, he had to give me a month. A month, and everything would be OK.

'All right, Savè, a month, but only because it's you.'

I didn't know what to do, I didn't know where to get the money.

Then my father died suddenly. That was the last opportunity life ever gave me. I sold the pastry shop. I managed to pay off my debts and even had a bit left over. But the money went just like that. One rainy night, playing a hand of poker I'd fooled myself into thinking would make up for lost time.

After three months I was twelve thousand euros down, I didn't have a cent and there was nothing I could do about it.

'Savè,' the owner of the villa said to me, 'on your next trip, don't pay the guy.'

And he put a gun in my hand.

'All right,' I said.

But the truth was, I didn't really think I'd go through with it, I'd never get to that point, I'd take the consignment of coke and run, go and live in South America or the Caribbean or Australia, I still had the idea I could get out of it when I wanted.

I wasn't expecting someone to go with me. It was like they'd read my mind and knew I was planning to do the dirty on them.

Now what was I supposed to do?

Savè, I told myself, if you don't do it someone else will. And besides, the guy you're expected to shoot is no saint, he's just some piece of shit, the world will probably thank you. Do it this time and then you'll find a solution.

But there weren't any solutions any more. There wasn't anything any more. I just had to do what they ordered me to do. I made an effort not to think and just do it, waiting to do another line of coke, waiting to get high and stop having to think.

In the end my hands started to shake. I couldn't keep them still, I tried, but they kept shaking. I saw the sun breaking up and turning black, I saw a mouth opening and I fell into it, I heard voices calling me, Savè, Savè, and I put my hands over my ears so as not to hear them.

So that was the end of it with me and guns. I wasn't good for anything any more, not even shooting a guy. I didn't have any way of earning money. I didn't have the money to score, and without coke I couldn't live. I thought

I was going mad, I felt like someone was pulling the guts out of me, and I threw myself on the ground, hoping the owner of the villa would take pity on me and give me a hit for free.

'Savè,' he said, 'I want to help you.'

'I'll do whatever you want,' I said.

'Come tomorrow at ten, we're getting in a new consignment for testing.'

'But I don't have any money,' I said.

'Savè, I'm not asking you to pay for it; you're our guinea pig. You try the stuff out to see if it's good.'

Here it was, I'd reached rock bottom. I'd become what they call a *visitor*, the man they give a daily hit to see if he lives or dies afterwards. If he lives they know it's well cut and they can sell it, if he dies that means they've overdone it and they have to cut it a bit more.

So now I get up every morning and take the 157 bus. I sit close to the window, with my head against the glass. Part of the time I look out at the street, the cars passing, part of the time I sleep.

I get off at the terminal. I lean on the wall to stop myself from falling and drag myself to where there's an open space. I sit down in the sun or the rain, it's all the same to me, and I wait, leaning against a pillar, like the others. I wait for them to bring me the syringe, already filled, look for a vein that still has room, and put the needle in. And they wait to see the effect it has, and whether you live or die.

I look at myself in the mirror for a moment, then turn my head away and try to walk, try to get to the end of the day, hoping it'll be the last one, hoping God will have mercy on me and put an end to this whole crazy mess once and for all.

3

REMEMBER THE SABBATH DAY, TO KEEP IT HOLY

It was about half past six when I woke up. I don't really need to get up so early, but it's become a habit, and even without an alarm that's the time I get out of bed.

After my shower, I rubbed cream on my legs, to make them look smoother. With tweezers I pulled a hair out from under my chin, then dried my hair.

I started making coffee. Through the window, I could see there were no clouds in the sky. It looked like it was going to be a nice day. I had a cup of coffee with low-calorie sweetener, got dressed, took my trolley and went out.

I bought milk, a kilo of tomatoes, onions, carrots, celery, a little ricotta cheese, four eggs, a sausage and half a kilo of minced beef.

'So your Enzuccio's coming,' the butcher said as he minced the beef.

'It *is* Tuesday,' I said.

'Tell him to come and say hello.'

'I will.'

'In the bar, around six.'

'I'll tell him.'

Next, I bought two litres of Gragnano wine. I always leave it till last because it's too heavy to carry around with me in the market.

At home I put the onion on to brown. Then I added the celery, cut thin, two sliced carrots and the tomatoes, chopped. On the side, I sautéd the sausage without its skin, then crushed it and added it to the sauce. I left the sauce on a low heat, I prepared the mixture for the meatballs, with the minced beef, a bit of breadcrumbs soaked in milk, the egg and the parsley. I mixed everything well, made the balls as big as fists and put them in the sauce to cook.

It wasn't even half past eight.

I changed the sheets on the bed, cleaned the bathroom, put the leftover coffee in the pot and got the coffee maker ready again, to be put on when he arrived.

I phoned my mother to ask her if she needed anything. I was just about to talk to her when the entryphone buzzed.

'I'll talk to you later,' I said, 'Enzuccio's here.'

I pressed the button. I waited until I heard the lift coming up and opened the door. Then I did what I've always done ever since we got married, I hid behind the door. It seems a bit stupid, now that we're the age we are, but I think if I don't do it it'll bring bad luck and something terrible will happen.

The lift reached our floor. I heard the doors open, then his steps on the landing.

'Ciuciù, it's me.'

He pushed open the door.

'Where's my darling Ciuciù?' he said in that cheerful tone he always has. He closed the door. He pretended to look for me, still playing the game, and when he saw me he said, 'Ciuciù, what are you doing behind there?'

He put his bag down, hugged me and kissed me on the mouth.

Like every Tuesday.

Like every Tuesday for the past thirteen years.

He quickly washed his hands, then we sat down at the table to have coffee. After the coffee he lit a cigarette.

'Fantastic,' he said. 'I feel like a king.'

'How was the trip?'

'Fine, Ciuciù. I even managed to get two hours' sleep.'

'You do look a bit tired.'

'I didn't actually go to bed last night.'

'Did you stay in the pizzeria?'

'Till half past three. Then I went to Lorenzo's bar for a beer. And at five I went straight to the station.'

'Everything OK at work?'

'Everything's fine,' he said. 'Oh, the money's in my jacket pocket. Leave me two hundred euros and take the rest.'

'All right.'

'Is Francesca up yet?

'Actually, it's time. I'm going to call her now.'

I went into the bedroom to wake my daughter.

'Is Daddy here?' she asked, still sleepy.

'He's been here for five minutes.'

I went back in the other room.

'Is there any more coffee?' he asked.

'Of course! Do you want a bit of milk?'

'Just a touch,' he said.

I filled the cup, put sugar in and gave it to him.

'Have you spoken to Marco?' he asked.

'He phoned on Sunday. He said everything's fine and he may be coming home this weekend. He said to say hello.'

He drank the coffee with the milk. With the spoon he took the sugar from the bottom.

'I made meatballs in sauce.'

'I'm already getting hungry,' he said.

'To start, I'll make rigatoni with sausage and ricotta.'

'I'll have a shower now and then I'll go and get the bread and the buffalo mozzarella.'

'Wait a bit, Francesca needs the bathroom now.'

'OK, I'll have a cigarette while I'm waiting.'

He lit the cigarette.

'You told me you were cutting down.'

'I'm smoking less than a packet a day, Ciuciù. I hardly ever smoke when I'm at work, I don't have time.'

He took a couple of drags.

'Hi, Dad,' Francesca cried out, appearing in the doorway of her bedroom.

'Hi, sweetheart. Everything OK?'

'Everything's fine,' she said.

Then she went into the bathroom.

'Ciuciù . . .'

'What is it?'

'Come here, give me a kiss.'

I went close to him and kissed him. He stroked my bum and kissed me on the neck.

'You're OK, aren't you?' he said.

'Yes,' I said. 'I'm fine.'

After the shower, he changed and went out to buy the bread and the mozzarella. The bread he gets from his cousin's bakery, and the mozzarella from Signora Aucillo's, which is very close. To get there he takes the bus near our building and gets off after three stops. There, he has a walk through the neighbourhood, says hello to friends, buys what he needs, then comes back.

While he was gone, I laid the table. Then I poured the wine into the jug and made a basket of fruit ready and put the water for the pasta on the stove but without turning it on, because there was still time. He came back at half past eleven. He made himself nice and comfy on the sofa and started reading the *Corriere dello Sport*. He usually falls asleep when he reads, because he's still tired from the journey. Today was no different. With the newspaper across his lap and his head tilted to the side.

I looked at him for a while as he slept. I noticed that he had a new line next to his mouth. And the index finger and middle finger of his right hand were a bit yellower because of the nicotine. I also had a few new lines, I thought, for example the one above my knee, but I almost certainly had others I hadn't noticed. Maybe he noticed but didn't say anything, or else he really didn't notice, because he was too sleepy.

At midday, I put on the water and before I put in the pasta I woke him.

'Oh, I always fall asleep.'

'Maybe because you're bored.'

'No, Ciuciù. Because I'm happy.'

He stretched, and came up behind me.

'I'm happy because you're here,' he said.

He gave me a kiss behind my ear.

'Go and wash your hands, we're eating in a minute,' I said.

* * *

'This rigatoni gets better every time.'

'Enzù, it's always the same.'

'No, no, there's something special about it. Maybe it's the ricotta, or the sausage. It's better.'

'Would you like some more?'

'No, I'm feeling full already, I'll fall asleep as soon as I get into bed.'

'Then sleep a bit more now.'

'How can I sleep when you've put on that black Brazilian G-string?'

I laughed. 'Christ, how did you know that?'

'I know everything.'

He drank a bit of wine.

'Did you find a new room?' I asked.

'Mazzarella found one, we're moving next month.'

'Is it closer to the pizzeria?'

'No, it's in the building opposite where we are now.'

'Couldn't you find anything more convenient?'

'It's not so easy. The restaurant's in a tourist area, they charge an arm and a leg.'

'One of these days I'm coming up there to say hello.'

'That's great, we can have a good look round.'

'I'd really like to see the Colloseum.'

'Of course. The Colloseum, St Peter's, we'll see everything.'

He took two meatballs with sauce and a piece of mozzarella.

'Did Francesca say anything to you?' I asked.

'No. Should she have said something?'

'Didn't she talk to you about the course?'

'Oh, right, the English course.'

'I think it's a good idea,' I said.

'Yes, but going to England on her own, I don't know.'

'She'll be with a specially selected family. And anyway, she's paying with her own money.'

'But she's just a child,' he said.

'She's eighteen, Enzù.'

'Well, isn't that young?'

'When I was eighteen I was already making love with you.'

'Eighteen? Are you sure, Ciuciù? You looked older.'

'Eighteen. You were my first.'

He thought about it for a bit while he ate a meatball with a bit of bread dipped in the sauce.

'Anyway,' I said, 'I think she has a boyfriend.'

'Really?'

'I think so.'

'Have you seen him? Do you know him?'

'No, but there's a boy who calls every day.'

'What's he like? I mean, how does he sound?'

'Nice. Good morning, good evening, how are you, signora? He seems like a nice boy.'

'Let's hope so,' he said, with a serious look on his face.

I didn't want him getting all worried, so I changed the subject.

'How are the meatballs? You haven't said anything.'

'They're delicious, Ciuciù. Not even my grandmother made them as good as this.'

'Now I'm even better than your grandmother. You really do want to make me happy.'

'I swear it on my children's lives.' He kissed his fingers as if taking an oath. 'I've never eaten meatballs as good as these.' He put the last one in his mouth.

'You've eaten them all up. Are you still hungry?'

'Hungry as a lion,' he said.

'Do you want me to make you an omelette with the leftover pasta?'

'No, Ciuciù, just come here and let me eat you.'

He stood up and came close.

'Don't you want a coffee?' I asked.

'Later,' he said.

He slipped a hand inside my blouse.

Afterwards, he got into bed and fell asleep in a second. I lay down next to him and rested my head on his shoulder. I didn't feel sleepy, but I liked being there with him under the sheets. Feeling the warmth of his skin, smelling his smell, listening to him breathing. I wanted to enjoy him longer than I could, and I'd have paid good money for those few hours on Tuesday to never end. But they were passing; it was like he'd only just arrived and he was already about to leave, I was already starting to miss him.

After a while I also fell asleep.

When I woke up he was still sleeping. I slipped out from under his arm. I gave myself a quick wash, then cleared the table and washed the dishes.

At five I heard him get up and go into the bathroom to have a shave. I put the coffee on to boil, on a low heat.

Ten minutes later he was dressed and ready to go out.

'I'm just going out for a walk, Ciuciù.'

'The coffee's nice and hot.'

He drank the coffee, put a cigarette in his mouth and grabbed his jacket.

'See you later,' he said.

He kissed me on the forehead and went out.

Like every Tuesday afternoon.

He'd say hello to his sister over there in the shop, then he'd go to the bar where his friends were. He'd have a coffee and a sambuca with them, they'd talk a bit about football, lay bets for Sunday's games, then say goodbye and go their separate ways.

In the meantime I took his dirty clothes out of his bag and put in clean ones. The white T-shirts, the trousers, the overalls, plus a jar of those aubergines in oil that he's mad about.

* * *

'Here I am,' he said when he came back at seven.

While I was making the omelette with the leftover pasta, he watched a bit of television.

Then we sat down to have dinner.

'Zuppetta had an operation,' he said.

'Oh, I'm sorry.'

He's known Zuppetta since they were children, and I know he's very fond of her.

'What's wrong with her?' I said.

'Something bad.'

'Let's hope she's OK.'

'Poor thing,' he said. 'I'll go and see her next Tuesday.'

For a while we ate without talking.

'Did you ask if they'll give you your holiday in August this year?'

'I asked,' he said. 'We'll have to see.'

'It's been thirteen years,' I said, 'they should give it to you at least once.'

'It might be possible if they can find a replacement. They're looking for one. We'll just have to wait and see.'

'Every year we have to wait and see.'

'I know, we just have to be patient, Ciuciù, and anyway I saw Gigio.'

'Oh, good. When was that?'

'He dropped by on Monday to get his things and talk to the owner and settle his accounts.'

'Is he going to open his restaurant in Fuorigrotta?'

'Oh yes, he's already in negotiation. He'll get going in two or three months.'

'And did you ask him if he'll take you?'

'He talked to me himself. He's going to see how it goes the first year, and if it goes well he'll make me his partner.'

'If only,' I said.

'Is there any more beer?' he asked.

'I'll get it for you.'

'Don't worry, I'll do it.'

He took the beer from the fridge and filled his glass and drank half of it.

'Do you want this other piece of the omelette?' I asked.

'What's Francesca going to eat when she gets back?'

'Francesca's going to the cinema. She'll eat out.'

'Did you tell her not to come back late?'

'Yes, I told her.'

'In that case, I'll finish it. Do you want any?'

'No, I'm fine.'

He ate the rest of the omelette. Then he lit a cigarette.

Tuesday evening is always like this. Compared with the morning we're a lot quieter; in fact we hardly say a word.

'I put clean clothes in your bag.'

'Oh, good. Did you put in the jar of aubergines?'

'How could I forget?'

'Where would I be without you?'

We watched television for half an hour, then went to bed because he has to get up at four in the morning to get to Rome on time.

'Enzù . . .' I said in the dark.

'Ciuciù . . .'

'Are you still awake?'

'Yes . . . What is it?'

'I was thinking . . .'

'What about?'

'Now that we've paid off the mortgage, and the children are grown . . .'

'Yes?'

'Why don't you look for a job here?'

'I am looking, Ciuciù, but the only jobs there are pay peanuts, you know that.'

'Then maybe I can get a job too, maybe if you find a pizzeria I could work there as a waitress.'

'Maybe in a couple of years, Ciuciù, when we've got a bit of money put aside.'

'You always say that, Enzù.'

'We need the money.'

'Yes, I know. But I want to spend more time with you.'

'We have time for that, don't worry, now go to sleep, Ciuciù, it's late.'

I heard his breathing getting slower, and after two minutes he was out like a light.

I couldn't get to sleep.

All I could do was think.

He was forty-seven years old, and I was forty-three. We'd been living like this for thirteen years. Seeing each other only on Tuesdays. Just so we could pay the mortgage and provide for the kids as they grew. But now the mortgage was almost entirely paid off. And the kids were grown. They were working now, making a living for themselves. I know there's never enough money. But I could look for a job. Anything. Just as long as he came home in the evening and slept in our bed. Just as long as we could spend one Sunday together every now and again. Go for a stroll somewhere, without counting the hours, without feeling that time was slipping through our fingers. A Sunday together, like everybody else. Maybe with him watching the match and me making soup. Watching a film on television. Playing a game of cards. Anything at all. Because I don't know what it is but I always seem to miss him more on Sunday. Maybe because everything's shut. And there isn't as much traffic in the streets as there is at other times. All you see are couples out for a walk. Some with children, some without.

A Sunday every now and again.

Instead of which, all we have is Tuesday. Just that one day, as if we've stolen it. Not that I'm complaining. He loves me. He works like a dog to provide for us. I thank heaven that everything's all right. But I miss him. He always says: let's wait a little while longer. But life doesn't last forever. One day you wake up with a pain somewhere and you end up in hospital like Zuppetta. And there's no more time to wait. Not even for Tuesday.

4

HONOUR THY FATHER AND THY MOTHER

Somebody had to do it. We couldn't go on like that forever.

Don Antonio would say I'm an animal, that it wasn't a Christian thing to do. But Don Antonio only ever set foot in here once, and even then he was in a hurry. He brought a bottle of limoncello, for show, and made the sign of the cross.

'Let us trust in the Lord's mercy,' he said.

Then he went away. He didn't even want to stay for a coffee. He made an excuse that he can't get to sleep at night if he drinks coffee, plus he had another visit to make. But you could see he was upset, that was why he didn't stop for a coffee, that was why he ran away. And he never had to stay up all night listening to her scream like an animal being quartered. He can make himself look good with words, but what do words matter anyway?

'Let us trust in the Lord's mercy,' says Don Antonio.

But that's all rubbish, it doesn't solve anything, only idiots believe that crap.

That's why someone had to do it. There's a limit to everything.

Two days ago she asked Michele, because Michele's older, so it was up to him. She thought I couldn't hear and she asked him. But I heard everything from inside the bathroom.

'Let's wait and see,' Michele had replied. 'Just a few more days.'

But I knew straight away that my brother wouldn't do anything, he acts hard but he doesn't have the bottle.

So this morning, when there was only me and her left, I said, 'I'll do it.'

'You're only thirteen,' she said.

But you could see she agreed. At last we could put an end to this hell.

'I'll do it, don't worry.'

She started crying, but with her eyes she said yes.

I didn't even know if I really had the stomach for it.

Before I did it, I closed the window, locked the door and drank two glasses of the limoncello.

I wanted to give her a kiss, but I thought I'd lose my bottle so I didn't.

It didn't take long. I thought it'd be harder.

Afterwards I put on the Nino D'Angelo CD she'd asked for and switched on the television and turned up the volume. There was a Popeye cartoon on. Olive Oyl was running away through the desert on those ridiculous little legs, and Bluto was following her on a camel and laughing. Popeye was tied to a railway track like a salami. He was trying to get free but couldn't.

What else did she ask me?

First, that I should finish at least the third year of high school. Then not to take drugs, not now, not ever. I told her she could rest easy about that, junkies gave me the creeps. All the same she made me swear. Twice. I swore. The last thing she asked me was not to quarrel with Michele. I told her I'd try, but you know what my brother's like.

'Try,' she said. But she didn't insist.

I drank some more limoncello and sat there in front of the television, not doing anything. I thought of calling Michele on his mobile. Then I dropped the idea, because there wasn't any hurry. I was feeling a bit dizzy, a bit drained like I'd just had a wank. The smell of fried peppers came up from the street. Inside, the smell of medicine was so strong, you couldn't breathe. Nino D'Angelo was still singing. The windows were closed, but the flies were getting in from somewhere.

Because of the music, which was quite loud, Rita came down and knocked at the door.

'Is everything all right, Ciro?'

'Everything's fine.'

She tried to open the door but it was locked.

'Let me in,' she said.

I didn't answer her.

'Ciro, are you all right?'

'I'm fine, Rita, leave me alone.'

She didn't say anything for a bit.

'I've made a macaroni omelette,' she said.

'I'll drop by later,' I said.

'If you need me I'm upstairs,' she said.

She knew something had happened, but she couldn't imagine exactly what.

A minute later I heard the key turning in the lock.

It was my brother.

He was wearing the same black jacket he always wears. And he had the usual nasty look on his face.

'What a shitty day,' he said.

He opened the fridge and took a beer.

'What's with the music?' he said. 'Turn it down a bit.'

I didn't move.

Bluto grabbed Olive Oyl's leg. She kept pounding him on the head, but Bluto just laughed. I don't think Bluto even likes Olive Oyl, he just can't stand it that she's always putting on airs. Olive opened her mouth and started screaming. Popeye was still struggling to free himself from the ropes but couldn't do it. A train came out of the tunnel with its whistle blowing.

Michele switched off the CD. He pulled the tab on the can of beer.

'What's there to eat?'

I didn't say anything. He'll notice now, I thought.

'So, little squirt, what's up with you today?'

As he walked past me, he gave me a slap on the head.

'You should learn some manners,' he said irritably.

I didn't say a word. I was waiting.

Michele took a sip of beer.

'Anybody ask for me?' he said.

I shook my head.

He took a cigarette from his jacket pocket.

'What's with all these flies?'

He put the cigarette in his mouth.

'Sure nobody asked for me?'

Again I shook my head.

Michele took a match from on top of the fridge and struck it on the zip of his jeans and lit his cigarette. He took a first drag, and that was when he finally saw her.

Up until that moment he hadn't paid any attention to her, maybe because the room was half in darkness, but now he noticed. The smoke blew across his face and the cigarette fell on the floor.

'What the fuck?' he said.

He said it quietly, as if he couldn't believe what he was seeing.

He went to the bed.

He looked at her, but didn't touch her.

Suddenly he started shouting like mad.

'What the fuck have you done, you fucking idiot, what the fuck have you done?'

His hands were shaking. His teeth were clenched and his eyes were all red with anger.

'What the fuck have you done?' he kept screaming.

His eyes came to rest on the television.

A can of spinach jumped out from Popeye's hat.

I heard Michele crossing the room, I heard him breathing behind me, then felt his hands grabbing my head and forcing me towards the bed.

'What the fuck have you done, you fucking idiot? What the fuck have you done?'

I looked at the bed and didn't say anything.

Looking now, I couldn't believe what I'd done.

Michele slapped me twice across the face. I didn't say a word.

'I'm going to kill you!' he screamed. 'I'm going to kill you!'

I touched my mouth with my hand and saw it was covered in blood.

'You're a wimp,' I said without thinking.

I remembered I'd promised not to argue, but I couldn't help myself, and anyway this had nothing to do with the promise.

Popeye was making an effort to reach the can of spinach with his pipe, but couldn't do it. The train was coming closer and closer.

'What did you say?' Michele said.

I looked at him for a moment. His eyes were narrow and he had his fists clenched together.

'You're a wimp,' I said again. I was quite calm.

And I looked at Popeye again. Popeye always escapes. He's never going to end up under a train, never in a million years.

I heard my brother open a drawer, and the noise of the cutlery filling the room. I could feel his mad eyes on me. Now he really is going to kill me, I thought. But I still didn't move.

'I'm going to kill you,' he repeated.

'You don't have the bottle.'

'You want to see if I have it? You want to see?'

'She asked me to do it,' I said, turning to look at him.

I looked him in the face. Eye to eye. I realised he didn't know what to say.

'What the fuck are you saying? What the fuck are you talking about?'

'She asked you too, but you didn't have the balls to do it.'

'Have you gone mad?' he said. 'What are you on?'

Now, with that knife in his hand, he looked like a complete loser.

'You're just useless,' I said.

'You want me to kill you?'

'Don't make me laugh.'

Olive was struggling like an eel and screaming silently with her mouth open, 'Help, Popeye, help!'

Popeye sucked in the spinach through his pipe. His body went all hard and the ropes popped away just as the train got to him. With one hand Popeye stopped the train.

I wished I could also eat spinach and become invincible. I don't know what I'd do, but it'd be good.

From outside came Totonno's voice. When he passes you can hear him all the way down the street.

'Fish, fresh fish! The best fish in the world! Come and get Totonno's fish!'

Michele threw the knife on the table. He held on to the can of beer until he'd finished it. Then he looked back at the bed.

Mum was lying on top of the sheets, not moving, with one arm hanging over the side as white as anything, and the pillow over her face.

Michele crushed the can in his hand.

'How did you do it?' he asked.

Popeye set off after Bluto, who was escaping on his camel. He soon caught up with him and with just two or three punches turned him into a cactus in the middle of the desert.

I heard Michele crying, quietly, so as not to be heard.

I remembered when I'd pressed down on the pillow and how she moved her arms. That was something I'd never forget, I thought.

5

THOU SHALT NOT KILL

I shot these seven or eight bastards who came running out of the forest with sub-machine guns in their hands and headbands around their heads; I blasted two helicopters and a petrol dump with my bazooka, and threw three grenades at the jeeps coming from the city, but by mistake I also hit an ambulance that was passing with its siren blaring.

'Not the ambulance,' Diego said. 'You lose thirty points.'

'Who cares?' I said. 'We'll still beat the record.'

Six tanks came out of the cave, bristling with machine guns.

'Shoot, Dad, shoot the tanks before they see us.'

I fired the bazooka and the tanks immediately burst into flames. The survivors came up through the turret and it was easy to take them out.

'Here's your coffee,' Rosaria said. 'It's already got sugar in it.'

'Put it on the table,' I said, 'I have to deal with these guys first.'

She put the cup down next to the computer and sat down on the sofa to watch television. But I'd got distracted, so when the ambulance passed I didn't fire.

'Shoot, shoot, that's the fake ambulance,' Diego said.

I fired, but it was too late, they'd already fired. The bunker where I was went up in flames and I had to come out into the open.

'Get away, Dad, get away,' Diego said.

I tried to run towards the half-wrecked church, and as I ran I sprayed bullets all around me with my submachine gun, I was running and firing all the time, but one of the bastards appeared on top of the bell tower and shot me twice with a precision rifle.

'They killed us,' Diego said.

'It doesn't matter, we've already broken the record.'

I dropped the controller and stretched my hand a bit, because it was half asleep from pressing the controller for an hour. Then I took the cup of coffee from the table.

'I want some coffee,' Diego said.

'It's a bit soon for coffee.'

'Please, Dad, just a little bit.'

'All right, it *is* Sunday.'

With the spoon, I gave him a sip.

'It's good,' he said.

'I'm just going to the toilet and then we'll have another game,' I said.

I finished the coffee, got up and went to the bathroom.

In the bathroom I moved the curtain a bit and looked down at the street. Everything looked normal. No mopeds waiting, no strange faces, nobody in the parked cars. The bar was closed and Don Vincenzo was walking his dog, just like he did every morning.

I flushed the toilet and washed my hands. While the water was running, I looked at myself in the mirror and saw my face staring back at me with a strange expression, as if it was taking the piss out of me.

'What are you looking at?' I said.

I turned off the tap, wiped my hands and lit a cigarette.

Rosaria was still sitting on the sofa in front of the television with her feet resting on the wooden stool.

'Everything OK?' I said.

She nodded.

I moved my hand over her belly.

'Not so restless this morning?'

'Apparently not,' she said.

Diego was fiddling with the controller, trying to start the computer without succeeding.

'Come here,' I said.

I took him in my arms, sat him down between my legs, and pressed the Go button.

'Dad, will you take me to Edenlandia today?'

'What is it, you already tired of PlayStation?'

The guys with sub-machine guns and headbands were starting to leap out from the forest.

'Look,' I said, 'I'll let you shoot this round,' and I put the controller in his hand.

'I want to go to Edenlandia,' he said.

I glanced over at the sofa and saw Rosaria looking at me.

'You promised,' he said.

I fired two or three shots, without much conviction. Diego wanted to get down, and he went and sat on the sofa next to his mother. He looked upset.

Rosaria gave him a hug.

'Daddy has a headache,' she said.

'He promised me,' he said.

I thought about it for a bit. Then I put out my cigarette in the coffee cup.

'We'll go in five minutes, go and get ready,' I said.

Diego started yelling, just like when Lavezzi or Zalayeta score a goal. He slid off the sofa like a spring and ran into his room to get ready. I just sat there in front of the computer, doing nothing. Then I looked at Rosaria. She was making an effort to keep her eyes fixed on the television and not say anything. All the while she was stroking the arm of the sofa with the palm of her hand.

'Don't worry,' I said.

She put a bit of the sofa cover in her mouth and started biting it, slowly, as if she was sucking it.

I went to the window and checked the street again. Everything was just as quiet as before.

'It's been three days,' I said. 'If something was going to happen it would already have happened.'

She was still sucking the sofa cover.

I went to her.

'Rosa . . .'

She turned her head away.

I put my forefinger and middle finger under her chin and applied a bit of pressure.

'Rosa, look at me . . .'

She slowly turned her head to look at me. Her eyes were watery but she was making an effort not to cry.

'I promised, Rosa, I promised.'

She closed her eyes and moved her head very slightly, as if trying to tell me she'd understood and agreed.

I put my shoes and my denim jacket on, put my dog tag round my neck, put on my dark glasses and grabbed my keys.

'I'm ready, Daddy,' Diego said.

'Let's go,' I said.

Before going out, without Rosaria seeing me, I took the gun from the drawer, checked that it was loaded and stuck it inside the belt of my trousers.

Diego got on the motorbike and held onto me. I turned the ignition.

'Put your helmet on,' I said.

'No, Daddy, it hurts.'

'Put the helmet on,' I said again.

'It's hot.'

'If you don't put the helmet on we're not going anywhere.'

He grumbled and put it on.

I let out the clutch and hit the pedal hard. The bike reared up. Diego gave an excited cry and held on even tighter. I went ten metres on just one wheel, then brought it down neatly and zoomed off.

As we were climbing through the streets, two or three people waved at us, but I ignored them. I was driving fast and making sure at the same time that nobody was following us. But there was nobody behind us. When we came out from the maze of side streets I also put on my helmet. I went along the Corso and through Vomero, and when we got onto the ring road I picked up speed.

'Are you scared?' I asked.

'Are you kidding?'

I accelerated even more.

From the top of the bridge all you could see was the emptiness underneath and the street moving straight ahead into the sky, as if we were going to fly at any moment, like a plane before take-off. The cars, unlike us, were going in slow motion, and when we passed them they made a noise like a whistle, or like a gun firing with a silencer. The wind was making my eyes water and I had to screw them up, actually close them for a moment, just long enough for them to dry, for the wind to take the water away.

'Daddy . . .'

'What is it, son?'

'Daddy . . .' he said again.

I heard a bit of a tremble in his voice and realised he was scared but didn't want to show it. So I slowed down.

After we passed San Paolo, I said, 'When I was your age and went to the stadium—'

'They had Maradona and he was something else. I know, Daddy, you always tell me that.'

'I always tell you that because it's true.'

'But Maradona's fat, he looks like a ball of ricotta.'

'He's fat now, but in those days . . . Nobody could keep him away from that goal.'

'You always say you're going to play me the DVD, and you always forget.'

'I'll play it today, after the game.'

'Promise!'

'I promise.'

I parked the bike. As I was chaining it to the post, I said, 'If you wanted, you could be as good as he was with the ball.'

'I want to be like you, Daddy.'

I felt a smile coming on.

'Like me?'

'I want to be just like you.'

He took me by the hand and pulled me proudly towards the entrance to Edenlandia.

The first thing he wanted to do was go on the roller coaster.

'Won't it make you feel sick?' I said, to pull his leg.

'What do you think I am, a girl?' he replied, offended.

'Only kidding. I know you're not scared of anything.'

He was quite worked up about it. When we'd got to the top and the car was starting to descend, to show me how brave he was he said, 'Look!'

And he stood up and held up his arm.

The little bugger almost hit me.

'Diego! Sit down!'

I tugged at his T-shirt.

He didn't react.

In the meantime the car had accelerated and was descending at top speed.

'Can you do this?' he shouted. 'Can you?'

'No, I can't, sit down!' I screamed. 'Sit down!'

At last he sat down. I saw that he was smiling and looked happy.

After the roller coaster he wanted to go on the galleon ride. I thought this time he was bound to feel sick, but I kept quiet, or God knows what he would have done. He has a stomach of iron anyway, because it didn't do him any harm, and if it had lasted a bit longer I'd have been the one with a dodgy stomach.

As soon as it was over he wanted to go round again.

'Go if you want, I'll wait for you down here.'

'No, if you won't come with me, I'm getting off.'

'Isn't there anything a bit slower?' I asked when we got off.

'The shooting gallery,' he said, pulling me by the hand.

At last something serious.

'But first I want chips.'

'Don't tell me you're hungry.'

'Why shouldn't I be?'

'Let's get some then.'

I took the rifle and positioned the butt on my shoulder.

'What would you like?' I asked.

'The teddy bear.'

'How many balls for the bear, darling?'

'Ten,' the girl behind the counter said.

I moved my eye closer to the sights.

'What are you going to do with the bear?'

'I'll give it to Mummy,' he said.

I nodded and took aim.

The balls were turning quickly round and round. I placed my finger on the trigger, aimed carefully, then started firing. One two three. The first three went down. One two three. Three more balls.

'Go, Daddy, go,' Diego said.

One two three. Nine were down.

'How many left?' I asked.

He calculated for a moment.

'One,' he replied.

'So you can do sums now.'

'I can count up to twenty.'

I pulled the trigger and the last ball went down.

He clapped his hands happily. The girl gave us the bear. She looked a bit pissed off.

'Do you want to have a go?'

He nodded.

I put the rifle in his hand and showed him how to hold it.

'It's heavy,' he said.

'Lean your elbow on the counter.'

He leaned.

'That's it, good. Now close your left eye.'

He closed his eye.

'That's right . . . When you feel like it, fire.'

He fired the first shot straight away.

'I missed,' he said.

'You have to aim to the left of the ball.'

He took aim and fired again.

'I can't do it,' he said.

'You can't do it because when you pull the trigger your hand shakes. You have to be decisive. Make a clean shot.'

He got in position again, took aim, without hurrying this time, then pulled the trigger hard and a ball went down.

'I got it, Daddy, did you see, I got it!'

'Good, you're a quick learner. Try again.'

He fired five more shots and hit two balls.

'That's very good,' I said.

We took the teddy bear and went and sat down on a bench.

'Do you want a Coca-Cola?' I asked.

'No, not for now,' he replied with a serious look on his face.

He ate the rest of the chips, and I lit a cigarette. As I smoked I noticed two young punks, no more than about twelve, but with tattoos on their arms, leaning against a tree, chatting.

'Are we going to the match next Sunday?' he asked.

'What do you mean, are we going? I've already got the tickets.'

I hadn't taken my eyes off the two punks the whole time. Maybe I was worrying over nothing, but I kept my eyes on them all the same.

'I hope it doesn't rain,' Diego said.

'Why should it rain? I'm sure next Sunday it'll be just as sunny as today, don't worry.'

The two punks started walking in our direction. They had their hands in their pockets and weird grins on their faces, you couldn't tell if they were smiling or in pain.

I put my hand under my T-shirt and placed it on the gun. Then I moved forward slightly in front of my son, so that I covered him almost completely. One of the punks said something to the other, who started laughing. With my thumb, I lifted the safety catch and waited for them to come closer. The punks took a few steps. One of the two stopped.

'The blonde one is mine,' he said.

'As long as she puts out,' the other one said.

And then they passed us right by and started chatting up two girls who were sitting on the bench just after ours. The girls said something in reply and the punks went and sat down on the bench next to them.

I took a deep breath, lowered the safety catch, leaned against the back of the bench and closed my eyes.

'Daddy, what's the matter?'

'Nothing, son, nothing.'

I stroked his hair.

'It must be the sun,' I said, 'it's as strong as anything.'

He ate another chip. A pigeon came and walked in front of us.

'When are you going to teach me to really shoot, Daddy?'

I don't know why, but I could feel a sweat coming on. Maybe it really was the sun, or the tiredness, because I hadn't slept for three days, or maybe the cigarettes. I'd been smoking too much lately.

'When are you going to teach me?' he asked again.

'What are you talking about?'

'I want to learn to shoot like you,' he said, 'with a real gun.'

I gave a half-smile. 'Daddy doesn't really shoot.'

'Oh, come on, Daddy, don't joke about it.'

I felt as if a hand was tightening around my neck, tightening so I couldn't breathe. The pigeon ate a bit of a chip. I took Diego in my arms and sat him on my knees.

'Do you like football?' I said.

'What do you mean, do I like it?'

'Do you want to play for Italy? Do you want to win the World Cup?'

'Of course.'

'And have you ever seen a footballer shooting guns?'

'No.'

'Then forget about guns.'

He thought about it a bit, then said, 'I want to be like you.'

'No,' I said, raising my voice.

'Why not?' he asked, also raising his voice.

'Because . . . Because . . .'

I couldn't think of anything.

'Why not?' he asked again.

A pigeon came and pecked at my shoe. I saw it had only one leg and hopped when it walked.

'Why can't I be like you?' he asked.

'Because I wanted to be a footballer,' I said. 'I wanted to, but I couldn't, and if you can be one, then Daddy will be happy and will love you even more. Now do you understand why?'

He looked me in the eyes.

I don't know how much a seven-year-old really understands. He nodded and gave me a big hug. And as he was hugging me, with his heart beating fast inside his chest, I could feel the cold gun pressing into my thighs, and I realised I couldn't do anything more for him. My one hope was that he never became like me. My only hope.

6

THOU SHALT NOT COMMIT ADULTERY

I waited for my dad to leave. I looked out of the window to make sure he wasn't coming back, then I took the plastic bag from under the mattress and pulled out the clothes I'd bought and laid them out on the bed. I took off my pyjamas and put on first my black cotton miniskirt, then the skimpy pink T-shirt with the rhinestones and the push-up bra underneath that makes my tits stick out, and then the pointed pink boots that matched the T-shirt. I put on a load of eyeliner and bright red lipstick. The mirror was small so I couldn't see the whole of me, but I thought I looked good, I thought I was exactly the way I wanted to be.

'What do you think, Monnè, how do I look?' I asked the toy cat peering at me from the pillow. Monnezza only has one eye, that's why you can never tell exactly where she's looking or what's going through her head.

I opened the drawer and took the money from under the scissors. I put it in my purse and went to the door.

'I'm going, Monnè, I'll see you tonight.'

As I was going out my mum saw me from the kitchen.

'Where are you going dressed like that?' she said. 'You look like a whore.'

I didn't answer her. I went downstairs.

Outside, it was hot and the sun was beating down.

On the main road the boys were playing the fool on their mopeds, showing off. Some were speeding, some were doing wheelies. They were weaving in and out between the carcasses of the fighting dogs and the mountains of rubbish. Backwards and forwards, like patients in a lunatic asylum.

As soon as I crossed the road they all zoomed towards me on their mopeds. Screaming like animals before they stopped.

'Rosa, been at the steroids again?'

'Rosa, where did you get that arse?'

'Rosa, want to give me a blow job?'

I didn't take any notice of them, just kept on walking through the dust they'd raised. I wasn't reacting the way they wanted, so they lost interest.

Debora was outside her house, texting on her mobile.

'Hi, Debora.'

'Rosa.'

'Who are you texting?'

'Marc'Aurelio.'

'And what are you telling him?'

'That I'm sunbathing on the beach.'

While she was texting, I wiped the dust off my boots with a paper handkerchief. Then I took out a packet of Vogue Lilas.

'Want a cigarette?' I asked.

'Maybe later.'

I lit mine.

Under the stairs there were three junkies shooting up. A mangy dog was wagging its tail behind a guy trying to sell a car radio. An old man passed by, talking to himself out loud.

'You look great,' Debora said.

'So do you,' I said.

I gave her a cigarette.

'No school today?' I asked.

'I'm sick of school. I'm going into town with Laura to look at the shops. Want to come along?'

'I have to get something for my mum. Next time, maybe.'

Debora's mobile rang.

'It's Marc'Aurelio,' she said.

'Aren't you going to answer?'

'I'll let him sweat a bit. I'll send him a message later that I was having a bath and didn't hear him.'

'Aren't you two together?'

'Are you mental? He's completely skint. I want someone who can treat me right.'

I shrugged but didn't say anything.

'Why, don't you?' she said.

'I don't give a fuck.'

'Then why do you dress like that?'

'Because this is how women dress.'

Debora finished her cigarette.

'Actually, you've been weird for the last few days, Rosa. What's up with you?'

'Nothing.'

I flung my cigarette away.

'Got to go,' I said.

'See ya.'

'See ya.'

The escalator on the metro was broken and I had to walk up two flights of stairs. There were lots of people on the train, and guys kept rubbing up against me in the crowd. Some guys do it just to touch you up, and some to find out where your money is, that's why I kept a tight hold on my handbag.

I got off at the last stop. I checked the address in my diary, but I didn't want to go straight there, so I decided to go for a walk. But walking on high heels knackers you and after ten minutes my feet hurt. It might have been better if I'd put on my silver Nikes, but it was too late now. I went into a bar and had a cappuccino and a croissant. There were two women sitting at a table talking. I sat down by myself and sat there quietly, just killing time. I saw the owner give me a look every now and again, so I crossed my legs to see how he reacted. He just looked even harder. When the two women went away and there was no one else there, he wiped his hands and came out from behind the counter.

'How old are you?' he asked.

'Seventeen.'

'Why aren't you at school?'

'They're on strike today.'

He came and sat down at the table next to mine and took out a packet of cigarettes.

'Want one?' he said.

'I don't smoke.'

He lit a cigarette and took a couple of drags.

'What's your name?' he asked.

'Natascia.'

'That's a nice name.'

All the while he was looking at my legs.

Another couple of drags, then he said, 'How about it, Natascia, want me to close the shutter for a bit?'

He winked and gave a kind of grin and I could see his teeth all yellow with nicotine.

'Do you have a daughter?' I asked.

'Yes,' he said. 'What's that got to do with it?'

'Then fuck her instead.'

He sat there not knowing what to say. I stood up and he started screaming that I was a whore, a slag. When I left he was still shouting. From behind the windows I could see his angry face mouthing something. I gave him the finger and walked away.

Outside it was even hotter than before.

I walked a bit more, in no particular direction. The cappuccino and croissant came up on me and I threw up against a wall. A few people passing looked at me, but nobody said anything.

I cleaned my mouth with a paper handkerchief.

A guy on a moped slowed down. I thought he was trying to grab my handbag and I jumped back. But maybe he only wanted to touch my arse, anyway he lost his balance and nearly fell off. I carried on walking, but I couldn't feel my feet and I looked for somewhere to sit down and rest. I passed a church. I could stay there for as long as I liked, I thought. Before I went in I looked at my watch, but it was still early and I wasn't in any hurry.

Inside there were only two older women praying, right at the front. I sat down on a pew and took off my shoes because I couldn't stand them any more. It was cool, it was a good place to chill. I sat there for a while, looking at the paintings. In one, there were lots of people looking desperate, just like people standing outside a house when they're evicting someone or someone has died. Another with a naked guy with lots of arrows in him, who looked exactly like Gennaro the junkie.

As I was looking at the paintings, a priest passed and glanced at me, then said, 'You do know this is the house of the Lord, don't you?'

'Yeah. And?'

'And is that how you dress in the house of the Lord?'

'Why, do you think God cares how I'm dressed?'

I thought he was going to say something nasty. Instead, he smiled.

'I don't think so,' he said.

I also felt a smile coming on.

'If you want to confess, I'm here.'

'No, thanks,' I replied.

The priest went into the confessional. I stayed where I was, looking around. I wanted to smoke a cigarette, but I didn't want to get into any trouble and I didn't feel like going outside, because I was all right where I was. I thought about things for a bit. Then I tried not to think. Then one of the old women went and knelt in the confessional. In the silence of the church you could hear their voices, but you couldn't understand what they were saying, like when you hear people talking outside in the street in the evening.

The old woman made the sign of the cross, then stood up and went out.

Suddenly I also felt like going and talking to the priest. Maybe just to get things off my chest. To tell somebody. Plus, priests keep secrets, so it wouldn't get out. Nobody would ever know.

I put on my shoes and went and knelt in the confessional.

'Do you have a sin on your conscience of which you wish to free yourself, my child?'

'No,' I replied.

I had the feeling he was smiling in the dark.

'Nothing to repent?'

'No,' I replied again.

He waited a moment to see if I was going to say something, but I didn't. I liked it that he was asking me questions. Like he was interested in what I had to say.

'Is there anything you want to talk to me about?' he asked after we'd been quiet for a bit.

'No . . .'

'Are you sure?'

'Yes . . . No . . . I don't know . . .'

'I'm listening, my child.'

I didn't say anything.

Tell him now, I thought. But it wouldn't come out.

Tell him now. But I didn't say anything.

'How old are you?' he asked.

'Fourteen next month.'

'And what could possibly be upsetting you at the age of fourteen?'

'I . . .'

I took a deep breath.

'I'm three months pregnant,' I blurted out.

The priest sighed.

'Who's the baby's father?'

I didn't answer him.

'Is it your boyfriend?' he asked.

'No.'

'Who is it, then?'

I felt like I needed air. I got up.

'My child . . .'

I ran towards the door.

'Wait . . .' I heard him say.

I opened the door and went out. The sun was even stronger than before and I had to close my eyes to get used to the light. Then I checked the address in my diary again. I crossed the road and walked as fast as I could.

The building was in a narrow, sloping street. There was nobody about. As soon as you went in you had to walk down a passage. At the end, on the right-hand side, there were stairs going down. I went down and knocked at apartment 7.

A girl who looked about twenty opened the door, you could see she'd been eating.

'Yes?'

'I've come to see Signora Fabiano.'

'What about?' she asked.

'About the diet.'

'Who sent you?'

'Friends.'

'Come in,' she said.

The room was a bit dark and smelt of alcohol. Apart from the hard bed in the middle with a sheet over it, it was a normal room, with a television, a sofa and a dining table.

'Have you got the money?' the girl asked.

I took the two hundred euros out of my bag.

'Here it is.'

'All right. Put it on the table and sit down. My mother will be out when she's finished eating.'

She went out. I put the money on the table and sat down on the sofa.

'What did you expect?' Signora Fabiano said, feeling inside with her hand. She had a hard face and half-grey hair covered with a hairnet.

'I only just found out.'

'Was it the first time?

'Yes.'

'Couldn't you have been more careful?'

I didn't answer.

'You girls just have to spread your legs, don't you?'
'Ouch, you're hurting me.'
'You should think twice next time,' she said.

Before getting the metro, I bought the medicines she'd written down. I was feeling a bit dizzy and confused. I couldn't wait to get into bed.

In the metro there were two guys sitting opposite, looking at me. Every now and again they'd make stupid faces or pass their tongues over their mouths to attract attention. I picked up a newspaper from the floor and made out I was reading. In the meantime I was starting to feel cold. It was the fever coming on, I thought. I'd have to take antibiotics until it passed. That was what the woman had said.

By the time I got out of the metro, the sun was going down. There were already plenty of people about on the street, looking to score. The guy who'd been trying to sell the car radio in the morning was still there, but now he had a video camera and was looking for someone to take it off him. Outside my building the junkies had lined up and wouldn't let me through. They must have thought I wanted to score too and was trying to jump the queue. Luckily it was Sandro who was selling; he lives in the building opposite and knows me, so when he saw me he shouted out, 'Resident!' and I was able to make it upstairs to our apartment.

I went straight to my room and threw myself on the bed just as I was. I wanted to take a shower to clean myself up a bit, but I felt so tired I fell asleep.

I don't know how long I was out.

The light came on and I woke up. Outside the window it was already dark. My dad was in the doorway, looking at me.

'Where have you been all day?' he said.

From his voice I knew he was already half drunk.

He gave that stupid smile and narrowed his eyes a bit.

'You look nice dressed like that,' he said.

I sat up and covered my legs with the sheet. My head was spinning like a ball, but the shivering had passed.

He touched himself between his legs and took a step forward.

I opened the drawer and took out the scissors.

'One more step and I'll cut your throat,' I said.

He stood there for a moment, looking surprised.

'Do you want to kill your dad?'

'Get out!' I screamed. 'Out out out!'

From the kitchen I heard my mum's voice: 'Rosa, what's going on? What's all the shouting?'

My dad finally went out.

I locked the door. Then I took off my boots, opened the window and threw them out. Then I switched off the light and lay down on the bed again and hugged Monnezza in the dark.

7

THOU SHALT NOT STEAL

I go up on the bridge over the valley, just before the sun goes down. I sit down on the little wall and light a cigarette. Below, the cars are passing. They're only going about two kilometres an hour because of the traffic. The horns keep hooting and the mopeds screeching up onto the pavement. All around, endless lines of apartment blocks. And the sun going down behind the hill, over towards the sea. You can't see the sea, but I know it's over there. At least I think so.

I've been coming here for three days now, always at the same time. I sit on the little wall and look at the cars and the apartment blocks and the sun and smoke one cigarette after another. And I don't know who to tell.

A bus has been at the stop for ten minutes with its doors open. People are shoving to get on; there isn't enough room for everyone but nobody wants to get left behind. Every now and then the driver tries to close the doors, but he can't, so the bus just sits there, with the cars going past at two kilometres an hour and the people shoving and nothing getting sorted.

Who can I tell? Pinuccio and Tonino, who don't understand a fucking thing? They're good for a laugh, they like messing around with girls, they can beat someone up when they have to, but they'd never understand this thing I've got inside me, never in a million years.

Who can I talk to then? Jessica? She's only good for a shag. She'd go blabbing to everyone and make me look like an idiot.

And even if I wanted to I don't know how I'd talk about something like this, I don't know where to start, I don't know anything any more.

Another cigarette. Waiting for the sun to go down. Waiting for it to get dark. In the dark, the thoughts don't seem to weigh me down so much.

Up until last week, I thought life was easy, I thought everything was simple. I thought all you had to do was put on a tough face, make your eyes go hard and wait for the other man to look away and you were sorted. I thought the trick was not to think about anything, because if you think you start to get scared. I thought that if I took my knife out everything would be all right, whatever happened happened, who gave a fuck? At the age of sixteen, I already had a name in the neighbourhood, Shank, because I wasn't too squeamish about using my knife, and one time when the motorcycle cops grabbed me I got away by stabbing one of them in the arm.

I snorted coke and acetone through a straw, I put a diamond in my ear, stuck a dog tag around my neck and I was fine. I could make five hundred euros keeping lookout, shouting 'It's raining' or 'It's sunny' depending on if the street was clear or not, waiting for the day when they'd ask me to shoot some idiot, and if my hand didn't shake, if they saw I didn't hold back, they'd know they could trust me and it wouldn't take me long to become someone who counts. That was what I thought. In the meantime Pinuccio and Tonino and me did a bit of bag snatching every now and again outside churches and monuments, where the foreign tourists are, especially Americans, who have more money and are easier to do, because they don't think anything will happen to them just because they're Americans.

Or else I'd fuck Jessica in the toilets of the bar.

'Be quick,' she'd say, 'my dad's coming.'

With her skirt pulled up and her hands on the sink and me behind her, pushing.

'I'll treat you like a queen,' I said.

But I didn't give a fuck about her. I didn't give a fuck

about anyone. Like when you walk in the street with a knife in your pocket. With your head in a daze because of the coke and the acetone. You go along thinking your own thoughts, wondering how to let off steam. You get to the traffic lights, and when it's red you stop and look the person next to you in the eye. And the thing you want at that moment, the only thing you want more than anything else, is for him to look away. That's when you feel good. You feel a kind of satisfaction that goes deep down inside you.

For half an hour you feel fine, you're not looking for anything else. Then the desire comes back. You wait for another traffic light. And every time you manage to stare them out, you feel really cool. Every time they drop their eyes you feel more powerful.

I didn't think about anything; there was nothing to think about, everything seemed ordinary, normal. I was taking life by the balls. I didn't question anything.

I don't even know his name. I used to see him sometimes taking his dog for a walk in the morning. At the same time every day. I'd see him from the window as he went out on the street. Wearing a shirt and jacket even if it was hot. He'd go along the street up as far as the crossroads, walking very, very slowly. He'd wait for the dog to have a piss, buy a newspaper from the stand, then go in the bar, buy a pastry and go back home. With his newspaper under his arm and the pastry in a little paper bag and the dog on its lead. At first, I'd sometimes notice him, sometimes not. A stupid old guy waiting to die. That was what I thought.

Then I found out about the pension.

I found out by chance, because of an argument I had with my mum about school.

Sometimes I go to school, mostly I don't. She says I have to go to school, that's the only way I'll get a good job and live a quiet life. I'll even get a pension at the end of it, like that old guy with the dog, and I won't be dependent on anybody. That's what she says, but she still takes the thousand euros I give her at the end of the month. She says it's cursed money and I'll come to a bad end sooner or later, but she still takes it. And doesn't even thank me.

I don't really pay much attention to my mum, I don't even listen to what she says, but what stuck in my mind was the bit about the old man's pension. Not so much for the money, because I was already making quite a bit. It was just a bit of fun, just to do something different, something that was all mine.

I started to follow the old guy.

Once a month he went to the post office, got his money and went home again. He always went on the tenth of the month. If the tenth fell on a Saturday or Sunday, or on a public holiday, he'd go the next day.

I thought it'd be a piece of piss. The man was old, what could possibly go wrong?

I studied the route he took, trying to figure out the best place and time.

The old man came out of the post office at eleven on the dot. As always. With his dog on a lead and the envelope in his jacket pocket. He crossed the road, stopped at Totonno's to buy a bit of fish, and while he was waiting for it to be cleaned he sat down in the sun with his eyes closed and his dog getting all restless because of the smell of fish. Then, when the fish was ready, he stood up, took the paper cone and went on his way.

I waited for him to turn into our street, pass the row of dustbins and go under the bridge. It was darker there, and I didn't think there'd be anybody about.

I don't think he heard me. In a second, I was behind him. I didn't even take out my knife.

'Give me the money,' I said.

That was all.

'Give me the money.'

I wasn't expecting any trouble. He was an old man.

The old man looked at me for a moment. Then he carried on walking, slowly, without any hurry. He didn't take any notice of me. Nor did the dog.

It was like I didn't exist.

Maybe he was deaf, I thought, or else a bit mad. I took

a few steps and placed myself in front of him. I pulled out my knife.

'Give me the money,' I said again.

I looked him in the eyes, with a really hard look on my face. I was waiting for him to look down, or start yelling, or pee himself with fear.

The dog started barking.

'Be a good boy, Frick,' he said.

He pulled a bit on the lead and the dog quietened down.

'Let's not waste time,' I said.

He didn't move.

He gave a kind of sarcastic smile.

'What do you want with my money?'

By now I was getting a bit nervous. I looked around, to see if anyone was coming. We were alone. Just him and me and the dog.

'What is it, you tired of living?' I said.

The old man pushed me aside with his arm and started walking again. He pushed me aside like I was a fly speck, like I was the brim of his hat. I was so angry, my heart was pounding, and the hand holding the knife was shaking. It was shaking and I couldn't stop it.

I went after him and stabbed him in the side, from behind. For a moment I left the knife inside him, then pulled it out.

The old man stopped. He didn't moan. Then he turned

and looked at me. Without saying a word. I can't describe that look. I quickly reached out my hand towards his pocket and took the envelope. The old man grabbed my hand with his. He had a strong grip. I hadn't expected it to be so strong.

'Let go of me,' I said.

He kept squeezing. So I stabbed him again, in the stomach this time. The dog started barking. I yanked my hand away. The paper cone with the fish fell on the ground and opened and the anchovies went everywhere. The dog was still barking. And the old man was still staring at me. He looked mad.

I took a step back, stuck the envelope with the money in my trousers and walked away. I wanted to run, but I forced myself to walk slowly. I wiped the knife on my T-shirt and put it in my pocket. Before turning onto the street I looked back.

The old man was still standing there with his shirt getting all red with blood and the dog barking and the anchovies on the ground.

I didn't go straight home. It wouldn't take long for the police to find me, I thought. I'd been stupid not to kill him. If I'd killed him that would have been the end of it, but now they were certain to come for me. And I'd have to do four or five years inside. Not that I gave a fuck, I was going to end up inside sooner or later anyway, and when I came out I'd have a name and people would respect me even more.

So I didn't give a fuck if they arrested me.

I bought a box of pastries and a bottle of champagne, I called Pinuccio and Tonino and we had a bit of a binge. They wanted to know what we were celebrating, but I didn't answer them because I didn't feel like explaining. In the afternoon I bought a pair of gold earrings, I went to the bar and gave them to Jessica as a present. Then I fucked her in the toilets. I did her twice. I felt angry inside like a wounded animal.

I got home at midnight, expecting the police to be there, or that they'd come looking for me while I was out. But there was nobody there except my mother, and she was fast asleep. And if she was asleep, that meant everything was OK.

The old man was taken to hospital in a coma. I heard it on the TV news the next morning. They said the old man had been robbed, and during the robbery he'd been stabbed twice. By the time the ambulance arrived, the old man was already in a coma. They showed the street outside our house, they interviewed a few people, but nobody had seen anything.

So they didn't know about me.

If the old man died I'd be fine.

But it wasn't certain he was going to die, there was still a possibility he'd pull through.

The next morning I went to the church of the Carmine. My mum always went there when Dad had his illness. Sometimes I went with her, though I was just a kid and don't remember much about it.

I lit a candle and put ten euros in the charity box. I looked round to see if there was anybody there that I knew. Then I knelt and looked at the Madonna with the baby in her arms.

'Please let him die,' I said. 'He's already quite old, he's had his life, so it's better for everyone if he dies.'

I didn't think that was enough.

I needed to say more.

'If you let him die,' I said, 'I'll give you all the money from the old man's pension. And even the money I make this week when I keep lookout. I'll put it in the charity box. It's almost one thousand five hundred euros. Let him die.'

I made the sign of the cross and went out.

The next day I watched the TV news again, to see if they mentioned the old man, to see if he had died. But they didn't say a word about him.

During the time the old man was in a coma, I still hadn't got it. I mean, I was a bit confused because I'd lost control, because I hadn't kept my cool during the robbery. But I thought that was all it was. At least that's what I thought. I saw Pinuccio and Tonino and did the usual things with them, every now and again I fucked Jessica. I did coke and acetone, and at traffic lights I'd stare out the people standing next to me, waiting for them to look away. But something wasn't working the way it used to. I could feel it in my stomach. And I didn't understand why. I thought it was because the old man might come out of his coma and give my name. And then they'd arrest me. I thought that was why I was feeling so uncomfortable. I thought it was all the waiting.

Three weeks later I was having breakfast in the kitchen. It was quite hot and I was in my pants and still sleepy. I was dipping the bread in the milk, not thinking about anything. It must have been nine o'clock. My mother had already left and I was alone in the apartment. That was when I saw the old man in the street. With the dog on its lead. He went down the street as far as the crossroads and stopped for the dog to have a piss. While he was waiting for the dog to have its piss, I got the feeling he was looking at the window where I was. It was only a moment. Maybe it was just my obsession, I don't know.

But I was convinced he was looking.

If the old man had recovered, I thought, then the police must know the robbery was down to me. But if they knew, why hadn't they come for me? Maybe the old man couldn't remember anything after he came out of the coma. That was possible. Or maybe he was too scared to give my name? That was possible too. But I didn't want to just hang around waiting. I had to know. I had to be sure how things stood.

I put on my trousers and T-shirt and went down into the street. It was hot and I was sweating, but I knew I wasn't only sweating because of the heat. I saw the old man coming out of the bar with the pastry in a paper bag. He was walking slowly in my direction. He didn't see me until he was two or three metres from me. The dog immediately started barking. The man looked up and saw me. The dog looked like it wanted to eat me.

'Down, Frick,' the old man said.

The dog stopped barking, but kept on growling.

As soon as he saw me I knew he remembered me. I was expecting him to be scared, or else that he'd give me an angry look. But he wasn't scared and he wasn't angry. It was a look I'd never seen. I never saw it at the traffic lights, or at the disco, I never saw it in the guys who paid me to keep lookout, I never saw it anywhere.

I forced myself to keep looking at him, but it was an effort. I wanted to drop my eyes, but not because I was scared, not that. I didn't know why.

'Do you still need money?' the old man said.

He said it softly. It wasn't a threat.

I shook my head. Then I couldn't stand it any more and I turned away, almost running.

Another cigarette. On the bridge over the valley. Below, the traffic is so heavy, the cars have stopped moving. The horns are blaring, but it's pointless. Only the mopeds manage to get up on the pavements. The bus has set off with its doors open and the people half in and half out. The sun has gone down behind the hill and sky has turned red, like blood. Slowly the lights come on, first the lights of the cars, under the bridge, then the apartment blocks, and then the ones further away, towards the hill.

I've been coming here for three days now. I look at the cars and the buildings and the sun and I smoke one cigarette after another and I don't know who to tell. I don't even know how to talk about something like this. I don't know where to start, I don't know anything any more.

I used to think everything was easy, everything was simple. I used to think there were two kinds of people in the world, those who lower their eyes and those who don't. The idiots, who are the majority, and the hard men, who get whatever they want because they aren't scared of anything.

But things aren't like that now.

And I don't know what to do. I don't know what to think any more.

8

THOU SHALT NOT BEAR FALSE WITNESS

I got to the square about seven. I parked my Mercedes by the self-service petrol station and got out.

I didn't recognise him at first. He was standing under the platform roof, all tanned, with his hair almost completely shaved off but with a thick beard and a scarf tied around his neck, the kind the Arabs wear, I think.

'Riccà!' I yelled.

He turned in my direction.

'Riccà, is that you?'

'Nicò,' he said.

He came towards me. We looked at each other for a moment. His smile was exactly the same as always. I gave him a big hug.

'God, it's good to see you,' I said.

'I missed you,' he said.

'How long has it been?'

'Nearly three years,' he said.

We hugged again.

'It seems like only yesterday that you left,' I said.

'To me it's like another life.'

'Come on, get in.'

'I bet this beauty never breaks down,' he said as he got in.

'She's old but who cares? She's done nearly two hundred thousand kilometres and still goes like a Swiss watch.'

'You can't beat the old ones,' he said. 'Where are you taking me?'

'Pizza OK?'

'I tell you what I really fancy, a proper spaghetti with mussels.'

'We can have spaghetti with mussels, no problem.'

'It's been three years since I last saw a bit of fish. Do you mind?'

'Riccà, today you're the boss. Let's go to Rafele's. You remember Rafele's, don't you?'

'Of course I remember it! Is it still there?'

'Who'd ever get rid of it?'

I started the car and we headed into the traffic.

'So,' he said, 'what's new with you?'

'What's new? Nothing much. I'm working. The kids are growing.'

'You have three now.'

'That's right, you were already over there when Luca was born.'

'Marisa said in her letter that you'd have preferred a girl.'

'Yes, but I really don't mind a boy. Maybe we'll try again in a while. How's your girl?'

'You should see how she's grown. She's already a little lady.'

'You think I haven't seen her? She's really lovely, she looks like you.'

'Poor her,' he said.

'What are you talking about?'

'Luckily she takes after Marisa.'

'She has your smile, though.'

'Thank God it's only the smile.'

For a while we didn't say anything. We were doing two kilometres an hour along the Corso.

'The traffic's worse than ever,' he said.

'And it's only Thursday. On Fridays and Saturdays, you can't move.'

After a bit, he said, 'You know something, you've put on a bit of weight.'

'That's what Luisa keeps telling me. I should go on a diet. But you, you're like a rock.'

'That's because you don't get a minute's rest over there.'

'What's it like in Afghanistan? Tell me all about it.'

'What's it like? Bad, really bad.'

'But is it quiet, or is it dangerous?'

He nodded. 'It's a war, Nicò, they call it a peace mission, but it's still a war.'

'Right.'

'And I was wounded once.'

'Really? I didn't know that.'

'Because I didn't tell Marisa everything. I didn't want to worry her, you know.'

'Of course not, that's only natural. Where were you wounded?'

He pulled his scarf down a bit. 'Here in the shoulder, can you see?'

I glanced over and saw the scar that went from his arm all the way up to the throat.

'That's one hell of a cut,' I said.

'It's not too bad, it's only a surface wound. But it scared me at the time.'

'How did it happen?'

'A fragment from a grenade as we went by in the lorry. A couple of centimetres more and it would have been goodbye Riccardo.'

'When it's your turn to go . . .'

'You said it.'

He lit a cigarette and took a drag.

'I saw a lot of people die, Nicò. Old people, kids, women,

and young guys like me who went there hoping they'd make a bit of money.'

I didn't say anything because I didn't know what to say.

'But there were good things too, don't think there weren't.'

'Like what?'

'The doctors who took care of us, for instance. Or when we took the lorries out to distribute food. The faces on the kids when we gave them chocolate or toys. That's when you thought it actually meant something, that it had a purpose.'

'It's the kind of thing that makes you grow as a person,' I said.

'You grow all right! I even grew a beard, see?'

'It suits you, makes you look more manly.'

'That's what Marisa said. But she says it prickles when I kiss her, she wants me to cut it off.'

We both laughed. In the meantime we'd reached Rafele's and I was looking for a parking space.

'How did you find Marisa?' I asked. 'All right?'

'I think she's more beautiful than before.'

'It's being away that does it.'

'Oh, I know that. But when you've been over there, you learn to appreciate the things you have.'

'That's for sure.'

'Everybody should go there for a year,' he said.

'For God's sake,' I said, 'there are already enough problems here.'

'Your work, right? Marisa mentioned that.'

'No, everything's fine now. I was just saying.'

In the meantime, I saw a parking spot that had just become free.

'Oh look, that's lucky,' I said, 'just outside Rafele's.'

'Can you get in? Are you sure?'

'I think you've forgotten who taught you to drive lorries.'

He smiled. 'I'm sorry, you're right. If it wasn't for you . . .'

I did a U-turn and reversed, getting in with only millimetres to spare. I set the parking meter for an hour.

As I was closing the door, this guy wearing a little hat with the word Mario on it came up to me.

'Mario will look after your car, signore.'

I was about to give him a euro, when Riccardo said, 'Why do you need to look after it? We've already paid to park it.'

'Sorry, signore, sorry,' the man said, giving him a resentful look. He spat on the ground and walked away.

'Wait,' I said, running after him.

The man stopped.

'What is it?' he asked.

I put my hand in my pocket and took out another euro. 'Here.'

I reached out my hand to show him the two euros.

'No, it's all right,' he said. 'You've already paid,' he added in a harsh voice.

'My friend isn't from round here,' I said.

He took the two euros. I think he was expecting me to thank him.

'What did you give him that for?' Riccardo asked as we went inside Rafele's.

'Riccà, you've been away too long.'

'Hey, young man, where have you been all this time?' Rafele said as soon as he recognised him.

'A long way away,' Riccardo said.

'And now you're back for good?'

'We'll see.'

'Where else can you go? Man is a domestic animal, he's best off where he was born.'

'Rafè,' I said, 'don't start getting philosophical on us, just bring us a drink.'

He brought us a litre of white wine. Then we each ordered a salad with octopus and fried whitebait as a starter, followed by spaghetti with mussels in tomato sauce, and for a main course marinated anchovies with broccoli rabe.

Riccardo poured the wine.

'To us,' he said, raising his glass.

'And sod the others,' I said.

* * *

The octopus was so good, it melted in your mouth. Riccardo sniffed it and ate the first mouthful with his eyes closed.

'I've dreamt of this for three years,' he said. 'Sometimes, at night, when you could hear the bombers going over, I thought I'd never taste it again.'

I could see his eyes were watering.

'Well, you're eating it now. Don't think any more about it.'

'It's great to be here with you,' he said.

'And it's great to have you back, Riccà, really great.'

We toasted again.

'These whitebait are amazing,' I said.

'They're a work of art,' he said.

He dipped a bit of bread in the octopus sauce.

'What did you eat over there?' I asked.

'Potatoes, rice, mutton, goat, stuff like that.'

'What's goat like? Tough?'

'I thought it would be, but it isn't, it's tender, quite tasty.'

'Was there wine?'

'No, no wine. Beer every now and again, when we could get it.'

'I couldn't live without wine.'

'You get used to it, Nicò, you get used to it.'

He dipped another piece of bread.

'I wanted to ask you something,' he said.

'I'm here, Riccà, ask away.'

Before he could say anything, Rafele arrived with the spaghetti.

'Rafè, you're the same as ever,' I said.

'I'm like my mother,' he said. 'One of a kind.'

He put the napkin over his arm and walked away to serve another table, walking in that exaggerated way he has.

'It's true,' Riccardo said, laughing, 'he's one of a kind.'

As we stirred the spaghetti, I said, 'Have you thought about what you want to do, Riccà?'

'That's what I wanted to talk to you about.'

'Are you looking for a job?' I asked.

'Later, Nicò. For now, let me enjoy my food, it'll cheer me up.'

'You're right,' I said, 'let's eat first.'

For the rest of the meal we chatted about stupid things, football, betting – in the old days not a Sunday passed without our placing bets – places to eat, friends he hadn't seen since he'd left. Things like that, nothing too serious, having a glass of wine every now and again.

When we finished with the anchovies, we had coffee and bitters. And we smoked, because there weren't many people there and Rafele told us it was OK.

'So, Riccà, you wanted to talk to me . . .'

'Yes,' he said, 'that's right, I did want to talk to you.'

He took a drag of his cigarette. He looked thoughtful.

'I haven't been back long, ten days give or take, so I may be getting it all wrong. But the thing is, I've been getting a strange feeling.'

'I don't understand. What kind of feeling? What are you talking about?'

'I don't know . . . But wherever I go, I feel like everything has changed.'

'What's changed? What do you mean?'

'I mean, in the neighbourhood, in the street. I get the feeling people have turned nasty, there are more problems, it's getting harder to make ends meet.'

'Well, it wasn't exactly paradise three years ago. Maybe you didn't notice, you were younger.'

'So you think it's just my imagination?'

'I don't know, Riccà, it may be.'

'I mean, like before, when we parked, the guy who asked you for money.'

'Well, it's always been like that.'

'I know, but it's the way he did it.'

'Riccà, everything seems the same to me.'

He sipped at his bitters.

'What it could be,' he said after a bit, 'is that because you want a quiet life, you don't notice any more, don't see things any more. It's like over there, in Afghanistan, at first you notice everything, every detail, maybe you can't sleep because you saw someone who didn't have any legs, who was walking on his arms, like a monkey. But then, as the days pass, you get used to the cripples and the bombs and the dead bodies in the street, you have to get used to it, otherwise you'd go mad.'

I poured myself some more of the bitters.

Maybe Riccardo was right. Maybe, like he said, to avoid asking myself too many questions, I'd stopped taking any notice of what was happening around me, the mountains of rubbish in the street, the murders, the bag snatching, the parking attendant who asks for money even when there's a meter. I'd got used to keeping my eyes down to avoid trouble, paying so that I could drive my lorry in peace, without them slashing the tyres or breaking the windows. Maybe it was like he said, but I didn't want to admit it.

'I don't know,' I said.

He nodded.

'Maybe I'm wrong, maybe I've been away so long, it's hard for me to get used to it.'

'Yes,' I said, 'that's what it is, you'll see.'

We asked for the bill.

I wanted to pay for the meal, but he wouldn't hear of it.

'I'm so glad to be here,' he said, 'that if I don't pay I'd feel like I was committing a sin.'

'God forbid. But it's my turn next time.'

'All right.'

'Promise you won't make a fuss?'

'I promise.'

'Young man,' Rafele said as we were getting up, 'I hope you're not going to go off again.'

'I don't think so,' Riccardo said.

'Remember, man is a domestic animal, he's fine where he was born.'

We walked out, swaying a bit and leaning on each other, because we'd already drunk two litres of wine. We even started singing 'Come Back to Sorrento', and then we started laughing, and it took ages to get the key in the car door, because we were laughing so much we could hardly stand.

As soon as we set off, Riccardo fell asleep. It was after eleven and there was hardly any traffic about. I drove slowly because I was a bit bleary from the wine. I opened the window a bit to get some air. In the sky, the moon looked like mozzarella, and you could smell the summer coming along. I checked my mobile to see if anybody had called and lit a cigarette to keep myself awake. I kept my eye on the road. I wasn't thinking about anything, but every now and again, without my knowing why, something we'd said over dinner would come back to me and make me feel strange inside, anxious somehow, and I'd immediately dismiss it, because I didn't feel like asking myself too many questions. When we passed the Nigerian whores I slowed down, because of the line of cars that were stopping to take their pick. Since you can hardly see them in the dark, they've taken to putting on orange jackets to be noticed. With their arses out and their orange jackets, I didn't fancy them, I felt more sorry for them than anything else, and I couldn't wait to get past the line of cars. As soon as the road was clear again, I accelerated a bit and noticed that the fuel gauge was flashing.

'Oh,' Riccardo said just then, 'I fell asleep.'

'Go ahead and sleep, I don't mind.'

He yawned and sat up to be more comfortable.

'What a nice night,' he said. 'It feels like summer already.'

'We didn't really have a winter this year.'

'It was fucking cold over there, Nicò.'

We passed a burnt-out dustbin. All that was left of it were the wheels and a bit of plastic.

'I've got a bit of money put aside,' he said.

'So you're in no hurry to find a job.'

He lit a cigarette too.

'You know what I've been thinking?' he said.

'What?'

He took a drag.

'I'd like to get away from here,' he said.

'You want to leave again?'

'Yes, but for good this time.'

'What are you talking about?'

'I just don't feel right here any more, Nicò. It doesn't feel like home to me any more.'

'What about Marisa and the kid?'

'I'll take them with me.'

'Where do you want to go?'

'I don't know.'

He took another drag.

'But I want to get out of here.'

'Have you talked to Marisa?'

'Not yet.'

'Well, you don't want to rush into things. Give it a bit of time and then decide.'

'Yes,' he said. 'That's what I'll do.'

'I need to fill her up,' I said.

We pulled into the service area.

'I'm just nipping to the toilet,' he said.

While he went to the toilet, I pulled the lever to open the petrol tank, got out of the Mercedes, put twenty euros in the slot, pressed the button and took hold of the pump.

I thought about Riccardo and how he wanted to leave. I thought it was mad for someone to leave the place where they were born, forget their old life, move to another town.

I put the nozzle in the tank.

But it also depends on a person's character, I thought. I'd never even left my neighbourhood. It's obvious I'm a domestic animal, like Rafele says. Someone who adapts to everything to get by in this city, and doesn't even have the guts to admit it.

I put the pump back in its place. Riccardo came out of the toilet.

'Maybe you're right,' I said.

'What about?'

'That you get used to things. Maybe it's like you said.'

I was about to say something else, when he screamed, 'The car!'

Before I knew what was happening, I saw him running towards the door of the Mercedes. I heard the noise of the engine coming on and saw Riccardo trying to open the door. I hadn't even noticed the guy who'd got into the car. He must have been hiding behind the van parked in front, or else behind the wall, I don't know, anyway I hadn't noticed.

The Mercedes jerked forward.

Riccardo was running after it, with his hand stuck inside the window trying to take the key out. I saw the Mercedes accelerating. Riccardo was clinging to the door and wouldn't let go. The Mercedes swerved two or three times to throw him off, but he held on tight.

'Let go, Riccà! I yelled.

The Mercedes accelerated some more.

Riccardo didn't let go.

'Let it go!' I screamed.

The Mercedes left the service area with the tyres screeching, skidding a bit as it went. It was like some mad animal.

After four or five seconds I saw Riccardo let go. He went flying a few metres, bounced once off the ground like a puppet, and smashed into the wall opposite.

Even though I was quite a distance away, I heard the noise.

Like when a dry branch snaps or you smash a wooden box with your foot.

He was lying in the middle of the road without moving.

'Riccà!' I cried.

I ran towards him.

'Riccà!' I cried again.

9

THOU SHALT NOT COVET THY NEIGHBOUR'S WIFE

'Adelina, why are you crying now?' I asked.

I tried the white shoe again, but it just didn't seem to want to go on. I stopped to catch my breath. Because I was on my knees, my dress was stretched tight and I was afraid it'd tear. I know I deliberately chose a tight-fitting dress, but since I chose it a good month has passed and in that time I've put on nearly two kilos. I'm careful about my weight, because fat runs in the family. Look how fat my sister Mariannuccia has got, and she's a year younger than me. She's like an elephant. Two kilos is nothing, fair enough, but two kilos here, two kilos there, and before you know it I'll be an elephant too. I took a deep breath, smiled at my daughter, but she was still crying, sitting there on the chest, with the tears rolling down over her cheeks like a fountain.

'Adelina, it's all right, it's happiness that's making you cry.'

With my hand I stroked her foot, then tried to get it into the shoe. As I was fiddling with her foot, I started sweating. It wasn't only because of the effort I was making. It was because summer had come early this year. A hot Sunday with the sirocco blowing. It was more than thirty degrees.

The sirocco was all we needed, I thought.

I wiped the sweat with the back of my hand and glanced at my watch. It was already half past eleven.

'It's getting late,' I said.

Adelina was still crying. It wasn't just tears now, she was actually sobbing, and because of the sobs she was moving a lot and there was no way the shoe would ever go on.

'You know I also cried that day,' I said. 'I really cried, Adelina,' I said, catching my breath again. 'It's happiness that's making you cry.'

It may well have been happiness, but she was still crying. Her tears had mixed with the mascara and were making her cheeks black.

'Adelina, that's enough now, you have to stop. You look like a gypsy with that black face.'

I'd raised my voice a bit. I could feel a drop of sweat trickling down between my breasts.

'God, it's hot!' I said. 'Have you seen how hot it is, Adelina?'

She gave a cry like an animal and put her hands through her dark curly hair. I'd spent a good half-hour arranging that tangled hair, and now it was wasted effort, now we were back where we started, but with her face all black, and looking like a gypsy, not the wife of Carmine Acciardi.

'Adelina, stop it, you're scaring me,' I said, raising my voice.

Someone knocked at the door.

'Donna Carmè, is everything all right? We heard shouting.'

'No, that was the television,' I said. 'Everything's fine.'

In the meantime Adelina had stood up, and was walking around the room, barefoot, with her wedding dress swishing over the white tiles and her clenched fists beating the air and her moans filling the room.

'Adelina, what is it, what's the matter? Talk to me!'

No answer. My daughter just kept on crying, like a bird that's been shot, with her clenched fists beating wildly in all directions.

'What's the matter?' I said again. 'Talk to me.'

She threw herself on the floor and started punching the tiles desperately.

'Get up, Adelì, get up before you make your dress dirty.'

She was like a wild beast. All sweaty, with her curly hair tangled, and her face black, and moaning like an animal, and her body shaking with sobs.

I went to her on my knees, also like an animal. I wanted to calm her down, I wanted to understand, and I was getting worried because in half an hour it'd be midday and there were lots of things still to do and this nonsense didn't seem to be anywhere near over.

There was more knocking at the door.

'Is the bride ready?'

'Nearly ready,' I said. 'A quarter of an hour and we're done.' But I wasn't so sure of that any more.

I tried shaking her by the shoulder. No reaction.

'Come on, Adelì, you really are driving me mad this morning.'

She let out a really exaggerated moan and I was so nervous I gave her a slap across the face.

In an instant, the miracle happened.

She stopped crying and started looking at me with those dark silent eyes that seemed to want to dig into me.

'Adelì, how do you feel? A bit better?'

She nodded.

I helped her up.

'Donna Carmè, the groom's here,' someone said from behind the door. 'He'd like to see his future wife.'

'No, no, he can't see the bride,' I said.

I was as sweaty and exhausted as she was, and scared that Carmine Acciardi would come in and see the whole thing. That was all we needed.

To be on the safe side I went to the door and locked it.

'It's bad luck to see the bride before the wedding,' I said.

To think this is happening to my daughter on her wedding day, I thought. The whole neighbourhood is here, even the Bishop has come to bless the marriage. At least now she's calmed down. But what could it be? The emotion of course, what else can it be, she's emotional. I remember, when I got married, my heart was beating like a hammer. But I didn't make a scene like this. Of course, everyone reacts in their own way. Anyway, the important thing is that she's calmed down.

'Come on, Adelina,' I said, 'let's hurry up, they're waiting for us.'

In the meantime I was trying to arrange her hair as best I could, because now she was finally sitting nice and still on her chair, with her hands in her lap, looking straight ahead of her as if lost in her own thoughts.

'Now let's try those shoes again,' I said.

I knelt again and started fiddling again with my daughter's foot.

'They must be a size too small,' I said, 'that's why they won't go on. But we're going to do it, don't worry.'

'I'm not going to marry Carmine Acciardi,' she said.

She said it very calmly, just as if she was saying that she liked her coffee bitter.

I almost had a heart attack. My hand shook and the shoe fell on the floor.

'Darn you, it was almost on,' I said.

I picked up the shoe and started trying to get it on her foot again.

As if everything was normal. As if I hadn't heard.

Maybe I'd got it wrong, I thought.

'There's no point,' Adelina said, 'I'm not going to marry him.'

I gave a quick push to the shoe and at last her foot went in.

Then I looked at her.

'Are you mad? Has your brain stopped working?'

'I'd rather kill myself,' she said.

'There's no need,' I said. 'He'll kill you. He'll kill your father too, and me, and your brothers.'

She didn't move. She just sat there, completely still. She looked like the Statue of Liberty, only mad.

'What's got into you today?' I said.

I cleaned the mascara off her face with a handkerchief.

'Mum—'

'Don't mum me. Carmine's your lucky break. He's rich. He's handsome. He's respected by everyone. He worships the ground you walk on. What the hell are you talking about?'

'I'm not marrying him.'

'If you didn't want to marry him, you should have said something earlier.'

I knelt again and fiddled with the other shoe.

'Let's get this one on and we're done.'

'I was scared,' she said.

'What?'

'I was scared.'

'Scared?'

'Yes. But I thought there was still time. I thought something would happen, he'd get shot, or be put inside, or else he'd go off me.'

'Adelì, it's too late for this now.'

'Then I'll kill myself.'

I don't know how, but there in her hands was a pair of scissors. She threw her head back and put the point of the scissors to her throat, just where you can see the pulse beating.

What a bloody awful day, I thought.

'Adelì . . .'

'I'll kill myself,' she said again.

And she pressed the scissors to her throat. Just a touch, just enough for a drop of blood to come out.

'Adelì, stop it!'

'I'm going to kill myself, I told you.'

'Let's talk about this.'

'There's nothing to talk about.'

'Then let's see what your father says.'

'If you call Dad I'll kill myself right now,' she said, and she pressed the scissors a bit harder into her throat.

'All right, keep calm, I won't call anyone. But put down those damn scissors.'

'I'm not going to put them down.'

'All right, don't put them down, but keep calm.'

I was sweating like anything. I sat down facing my daughter and wiped the sweat with a piece of kitchen towel.

'Adelì, tell me what this is all about, or I'll go as mad as you.'

She didn't say anything, just sat there with the scissors in her hand, ready for anything.

'Why don't you want to marry him?'

'I don't want to marry him, and that's that.'

'Is there someone else?'

She didn't answer me.

'Is that it, there's someone else?'

'Yes, there's someone else. What difference does it make?'

'Oh, no difference, one corpse more, one corpse less . . .'

'I'm not going to marry him, make some excuse.'

'What kind of excuse, Adelì?'

'I don't know. I hear voices, I've lost my voice, I want to become a nun. Yes, that's it, I'm becoming a nun. That'll do.'

I closed my eyes. My head was starting to hurt and I didn't know what to do.

'And who is this other man?' I asked, just to gain time.

Adelina didn't answer me.

I was starting to get curious.

'Who is he? What kind of work does he do?'

'Honest work, that's for sure.'

'All right, I get it. What does he do?'

'He's at sea.'

'He's what?'

'He's at sea, he's a sailor.'

Just like me when I was her age, I thought.

'Adelì, listen to me. You're going to marry Carmine Acciardi now. Once he's over the excitement of the first few months your husband'll lose interest, you'll be free and you can sleep with whoever you like, your sailor, the plumber, whoever you like. You just have to be careful. That's how it's always worked, and that's why we women haven't done too badly for ourselves.'

'Is that how it was with you and Dad?'

I looked her in the eyes. I raised my hand to give her a slap. But I controlled myself and stroked her hair instead.

'Leave your father out of it.'

'That was it, wasn't it? You didn't love Dad. You only married him because it was convenient for you, because of the money.'

'You don't know anything.'

'What's there to know, what's there to understand?'

'Adelì, now's not the time.'

'I don't want to end up like you.'

'What do you want to do, start a revolution?'

'I'm not marrying that man, don't you understand?'

And again she held the scissors to her throat.

I took a deep breath and stood up and walked around the room. I wanted to tell her that there was nothing special about the way I ended up, it was just the way the world works. A sailor! Life really is strange. I felt a smile coming on. I looked at my watch. It was already ten to twelve. There was no more time to talk. What a bloody awful day, I thought again.

I also thought I needed to find a solution. Any solution.

'Let's say you're paralysed.'

Adelina looked at me. Silent. Waiting for the rest.

'You had an epileptic fit and now you can't feel your legs. You're scared. Your head hurts. You can't even remember your name. We have to rush you to hospital.'

'And when we get to the hospital?'

'Then we'll see.'

'All right,' she said.

'Are you sure?'

She nodded.

I went to the door and turned the key. Then I turned to look at my daughter. She was already lying on the floor, shaking a bit and kicking her legs, as if she were having convulsions.

I made the sign of the cross.

I screamed, twice.

Then I threw the door open and ran outside screaming, 'Help! Help me! Help me! Adelina! What a terrible thing! Jesus, Mary and Joseph, what a terrible thing! Help! Help me! Adelina! What a terrible thing!'

I knelt on the landing and tore my hair and beat my head against the wall.

'Mary Mother of God! Help! Adelina! What a terrible thing!'

10

THOU SHALT NOT COVET ANYTHING THAT IS THY NEIGHBOUR'S

Panzarotto, Rolex and me.

Sitting on a wall, not doing anything.

Not feeling like doing anything.

Not waiting for anyone.

And no one waiting for us.

'Hey, man, how about getting some rolls?'

'Panzarò,' I said, 'your stomach must be really fucked, you're always hungry.'

'Fuck you,' he said. 'For that, I'll fuck your sister,' he said.

'You won't be the first,' Rolex said.

'Leave my sister out of it,' I said.

'Why, do you want to fuck her yourself?' Panzarotto said.

'Even if I wanted to, what the fuck is it to you?'

'Nothing, Ray-Ban, nothing, just having a bit of fun.'

'Go and have fun with your pig of a mother,' I said.

Panzarotto didn't say anything for a bit, just fiddled with his dog tag. Then he said, 'Well, I'm going to buy a roll. You two want anything?'

'Bring us a couple of beers,' Rolex said.

Panzarotto went into the pub. Rolex and I stayed outside, sitting on the wall.

'Bung me a cigarette,' I said.

Rolex passed me a cigarette and put one in his own mouth. He lit mine first, then his.

'Where should we go tonight?' he said.

'Where do you want to go?'

He shrugged. 'Just as long as we do something.'

'Let's go up to Vomero,' I said.

'Sounds good.'

Panzarotto came back with the roll and two beers.

'Here's the beer.'

'Eat quick, Panzarò, we're going up to Vomero,' Rolex said.

He nodded, and in two mouthfuls he finished off the roll.

We drank the beers, threw the cans in the road, and headed for the metro.

'As long as we get back early,' Panzarotto said. 'I've got work tomorrow.'

'Call that work?' I said.

'What do you call it?'

'Baker's assistant. That's for fucking losers.'

'Maybe I like being a loser.'

'Do what you want, Panzarò,' Rolex said, 'as long as we get out of here.'

It was nearly nine, and there weren't many people in the metro. The guy checking the tickets was standing in front of his booth. When we passed he said, 'Got tickets, boys?'

'Of course we got them,' I said. I put my hand behind me, on the pocket where I had my knife, and went right up to him.

'Want to see?'

Panzarotto and Rolex also moved in on him.

'Want to see?' they said.

The guy realised there was no point making a fuss.

'All right, go through,' he said.

We got in the last carriage, which was half empty, so there was room to sit. I sprawled with my feet on the seats, next to a girl reading a book.

'What is that, a love story?'

The girl didn't answer, just carried on reading.

'Hey, I asked you a question,' I said, louder this time.

'Yes,' she said, scared now.

'What's it called?' I said.

Panzarotto and Rolex laughed. The girl stood up and went to the other end of the compartment. An old man who was standing nearby said, 'Where do you think you are, in your own home?'

Rolex stood up, he wanted to make something of it. But I didn't feel like it.

'Let it go, Rolex. The guy's old. Another couple of days and he'll be dead anyway.'

'Did you get that?' Panzarotto said. 'You'll be dead by tomorrow.'

And he belched in his face.

'Uncivilised louts,' the old man said.

But he also changed his seat.

We got off at Piazza Vanvitelli. It was lively, because it was Friday; people were going for pizza, or out dancing, everyone was going somewhere. We walked around, just doing a recce, then we went into the bar next to the Diana Theatre for a beer.

'Your round, Panzarotto,' Rolex said.

'Why is it always my round?'

'He's right,' I said, 'he's a loser,' and I put a hundred-euro note on the counter.

'Don't you have any change?' the barman asked.

'I'm all out of change.'

He grumbled a bit, then checked the note to make sure it wasn't fake.

'What is it, don't you trust me?'

He didn't answer, just gave me the change.

'Aren't you going to give us any peanuts?' Panzarotto said.

The guy put a few peanuts on a little plate. But he counted them out, like he was paying for them.

While we were having our beers, this guy comes in. He was about fifty, with a jacket and tie and round glasses on a little chain and a newspaper under his arm. The woman he was with was wearing perfume and fishnets and a low-cut dress and she was so thin you could see her bones.

'She left her tits at home,' Rolex said.

Panzarotto laughed so hard he choked on the nuts and sprayed beer over them. It even got a bit of a laugh out of the barman. The man and woman didn't pay any attention. They ordered an aperitif. As they were drinking, the woman's mobile started ringing.

'Excuse me,' she said.

She walked over towards the door and started talking into her phone. The man opened his newspaper.

'Ask him the time,' I said to Panzarotto.

'I think it's half past nine.'

'I know that, but I want you to ask him the time,' I said, nodding towards the guy with the glasses.

Panzarotto went up to him.

'Excuse me, sir, would you be so kind as to tell me what time it is?'

He's really good when he does his polite act.

While the man was looking at his watch to check the time, I emptied the little plate of nuts into the woman's glass without anyone noticing.

'Nine twenty-seven,' the man said.

'Thanks a lot,' Panzarotto replied.

We stood there drinking our beer.

The woman came back.

'It was Guglielmo and his wife,' she said. 'They're just coming.'

Then she picked up her glass and took a sip.

'What's in this?'

'Where, signora?' the barman asked.

'In my glass. It's full of peanuts.'

'They must have been thirsty too,' Rolex said

Panzarotto and I made an effort not to laugh. The barman glanced at us.

'I'll bring you another one, signora, don't worry.'

'It's unbelievable,' the woman said, properly pissed off. 'What kind of world are we living in?'

We left the bar and walked around a bit more. There was a crowd outside a club, so we stopped too. We smoked and watched the girls going in and out.

'I'd do that one doggy-style.'

'I'd have that one on top.'

'I'd like to fuck that one on a table.'

'That one'd be good for sixty-nine.'

'That one's a dog, Panzarotto can have her.'

When we'd had enough of looking at the girls, we tried to get into the club. But the bouncers said it was a private party and you had to have an invitation to get in. We insisted but there was no way.

We'd hardly gone twenty metres when this young guy came running after us. He was wearing a white shirt and a bow tie. He was nervous and was twitching a lot.

'Do you want to go in?' he asked.

'We need an invite,' I said, 'and we don't have one.'

'I can get you in.'

'Thanks,' Panzarotto said.

'Why would you do that?' I asked.

He looked around for a moment, then said, 'There's someone after my girlfriend.'

'So your girlfriend's a slag,' Rolex said.

'You want to give your girlfriend a lesson, is that it?' I asked.

'Not her, him,' he said. 'I'll let you in and you scare him a bit.'

'All right,' I said. 'You let us in and we'll handle it.'

Inside, it was full of those fancy coloured paper things going from one wall to the other, with little balls attached, and lights like in Chinese restaurants. Two tables were piled high with little slices of pizza and mozzarella bites and salami and other stuff. There were three or four people up on a stage singing some lame Italian song. A few people were dancing, most were just hanging around.

'Would you like a drink?' the young guy asked.

We went to the bar counter and ordered three gin and Schweppes.

When the song finished, people started clapping. This other guy got up on the stage and grabbed the microphone; he was tall and thin as a nail, with spots on his face like he had measles or something and hair flopping in front of his eyes that he kept sweeping back with his hand.

'The next song is dedicated to Silvia,' he said.

'That's him,' the young guy said.

'What's his name?'

'Luca.'

'And your girlfriend?'

'Silvia.'

'Leave him to us.'

'Go easy with him.'

'Don't worry.'

'You just have to scare him,' he said.

'Got any gear?' Rolex asked.

'What?'

'Weed, coke, pills. Do you have anything?'

'Oh, yes. Hold on.'

He went through a door and after a minute came back with three pills.

'All I have are these,' he said.

'Is it good stuff?' I asked.

'The best.'

We took the pills and washed them down with the rest of the gin.

'I'm off now,' he said.

'OK,' I said.

He walked around a bit, then went and sat down on a sofa next to two girls and started talking to them. Every now and again he looked in our direction, to check what we were up to.

We had three more gin and Schweppes.

Two minutes later Luca went into the toilet. We finished our drinks and went in after him.

There were three doors with a picture of a man smoking a cigar on each of them. The toilet had green tiles and sinks with gold taps and mirrors with lights. Everything looked like it was out of a film.

'It's like the bathroom in *Titanic*,' Panzarotto said.

'You're right,' Rolex said.

I tried the doors of the cubicles. The first two were open and there was nobody in them. The third was closed.

'It's engaged,' a voice said inside.

'Panzarò, make sure nobody comes in.'

Panzarotto went and stood outside to keep an eye on the door.

Rolex went into one of the empty cubicles. I started washing my hands.

After ten seconds I heard the toilet flushing. The door opened and Luca came over to the basin next to mine to wash his hands.

'Hi,' he said.

I didn't answer him.

'Why are you wearing sunglasses?' he asked.

'None of your fucking business.'

'Sorry,' he said.

He went to dry his hands under the dryer thing.

'Luca,' I said, still washing my hands.

'Oh, do we know each other?' he said. 'What's your name?'

I turned to look at him.

'You have to do me a favour, Luca.'

'If I can,' he said.

Rolex came out from the cubicle.

'Yes, you can,' he said.

Luca looked towards the exit. 'What do you guys want?'

I took a step towards him. He was taller than me and my head came up to his shoulder. I adjusted my glasses with my thumb.

'You have to forget about Silvia.'

'Leave me alone,' he said.

He pushed me away and started towards the exit. Rolex

put his foot out and Luca tripped over it. I grabbed him by his jacket and pulled him towards me. Then we stuck his head under the water. He moved his hands to try and get free, but he was as weak as a girl and had to give up.

I grabbed his hair and slammed his head against the mirror.

'Did you understand what I said? Forget about Silvia.'

'All right, all right, let me go,' he said, snivelling.

I took out my knife and pointed it at his throat.

'You can see we're not joking.'

He was shaking like a leaf.

'Let me go,' he said, 'please.'

'Did you understand what I said?'

'Yes, yes, I get it. Just let me go.'

This was no fun. He was too scared.

I grabbed his balls with my hands and squeezed them.

'If you ever talk to Silvia again, I'll cut your balls off and make you swallow them.'

'All right, I understand, just don't hit me.'

I turned him round to face me. He was so scared I was going to hit him, his face was white.

'Don't hit me,' he said again.

If I let him go now, I thought, he'd walk out of the toilet and start screaming like a girl. I gave him a shove from behind and sent him crashing into the cubicle. He fell on the floor and lay there all curled up, like he was expecting a kick at any moment.

'You never saw us,' I said.

'Anything you say, please let me go.'

'Now I'm going to lock you in the toilet and you can stay there and have a nice quiet wank.'

'Don't hurt me, please.'

I locked the door and threw the key in the bin.

I washed my hands again and dried them on my trousers and adjusted my glasses, and Rolex and I went out.

'Everything OK?' Panzarotto said.

'Let's get out of here,' I said.

As we were walking through the club, Panzarotto grabbed a handful of mozzarella bites and stuck them in his pocket. The guy who'd let us in looked in our direction. We ignored him and went out.

'He was even more scared than you, Panzarò,' Rolex said while we were walking down the street.

'I'm not scared of anything,' Panzarotto said, already eating the mozzarella bites.

'Where shall we go now, Ray-Ban?' Rolex said.

My head was spinning a bit. The street lights seemed to be moving and the people had distorted faces, like in the cartoons.

'I'm going home,' Panzarotto said. 'I feel a bit dizzy, and tomorrow—'

'You have to get up early, we know,' Rolex said.

The street was moving from side to side.

'But we could go and get some pizza,' Panzarotto said.

'Are you feeling ill?' Rolex said.

'Look over there,' I said.

The three of us stood there, absolutely still, with our mouths half open, like we'd seen a ghost. It was red and shiny, and the engine was on and the rear lights flashing. It looked like something from a film. It looked like it was waiting just for us.

'Nice,' Panzarotto said.

'I'd pay to test-drive that,' Rolex said.

We walked slowly towards it, to get a better look. Inside we could see a man talking on his mobile.

The lights were still flashing.

'How about going for a spin?' I said.

'I wish,' Rolex said.

The only sound was the noise of the engine humming. There was nobody around.

'Panzarò,' I said, 'go and ask him for directions.'

'What should I ask him?'

'Whatever you like, how to get to the metro, how to get to some street or bar, just as long as you get him to talk.'

'Got it,' he said.

As he walked towards the driver's side, Rolex and I crouched down behind the car.

'Excuse me,' Panzarotto said. 'Do you know where I can find a metro station?'

I crept towards Panzarotto. Rolex went round the other side.

The man in the car gestured with his hand.

'Excuse me,' Panzarotto said, 'but which way is that? I didn't quite get it.'

I heard the noise of the window being lowered. I stuck my hand in my pocket and took out the knife.

'End of the street, then turn right,' the man said.

A moment later I almost jumped in through the window, with the knife in my hand. At the same time Rolex opened the door on the other side and slid inside.

'Get out,' I said.

The man was calm and didn't move.

I put the knife close to his neck.

'Get out,' I said again.

On the other side, Rolex was also pointing his knife at the man.

'You're making a big mistake,' the man said.

I opened the door slowly, then grabbed him by the arm and pulled him.

'Just move, get out of the car.'

I saw that he was moving his right hand under the dashboard so I brought my knee forward and hit him hard in the face. At the same time, Rolex stabbed him in the arm.

The man was half stunned. But he didn't moan or anything.

'Who are you?' he said. 'Who sent you?'

'Nobody. Just get out of the car.'

The man got out.

'You're making a big mistake,' he said again.

I headbutted him and Panzarotto kicked him in the balls and we shoved him so that he fell against the wall. Then I sat down in the driving seat.

'Get in, move,' I said to Panzarotto.

He got in and sat down next to Rolex.

'Can you drive this thing?' Rolex said.

'It's not that hard.' I pressed on the clutch pedal, went into first gear and slowly took it down. The car started to move. At first it sounded like it was sobbing, but then, when I stepped on it, it picked up speed and slid out beautifully.

'Go on, Ray-Ban, give it all you've got,' Rolex said.

I turned into the Via Cilea, because you can drive faster there, and pretty soon we'd reached eighty.

'Schumacher can suck our cocks,' Rolex said.

Ninety, a hundred, a hundred and ten. It seemed to be driving itself.

'Slow down a bit,' Panzarotto said.

'Why slow down? I wanna fly,' Rolex said.

I passed three cars, and put my foot down even harder.

A hundred and twenty. A hundred and thirty.

'You're going too fast,' Panzarotto said. 'Slow down.'

'I want to get to two hundred,' I said.

It really felt like we were flying. It was like your heart was in your throat and trying to get out, like you were invincible and nothing could possibly go wrong.

We took a bend at a hundred and fifty.

I heard the car skidding.

'Brake!' Panzarotto screamed.

I braked, but it was too late. The car hit some rubbish bins with its left-hand side, spun round, crashed against another parked car, and turned over twice. Then I didn't feel anything any more.

I moved my tongue over my lips and tasted blood. It tasted sweet. My left arm weighed a ton and I couldn't move it. But my right arm was fine and I could move my legs. My head hurt, but it wasn't too bad.

I opened my eyes.

The light was so strong I couldn't see anything. I put my hand up to my face, looking for my glasses, but couldn't find them. I heard a voice say, 'You must be looking for these.'

I squinted a bit and forced myself to look.

I was in a big room that looked like a cellar. Five or six metres in front of me a man was sitting in an armchair. There was another armchair, but it was empty, and there were four men standing there, with black jackets and shaved heads and their arms crossed. I tried to turn my head to the side. My neck hurt, but I managed to move it. I saw Rolex sitting on a chair. One of his legs was twisted at a weird angle, with the bone sticking out from under his jeans. His head was thrown back, and I didn't know if he was asleep or dead. I looked on the other side and saw Panzarotto, who was also sitting. He had blood on his forehead, but it didn't look too serious.

'Ray-Ban, where are we?' he said when he saw I was awake.

One of the men in black jackets slapped me across the face with the back of his hand.

'I told you you were making a big mistake,' a voice said behind me.

I recognised the voice. I thought it was better to keep still.

The man behind walked around to the front of the chair. His nose was swollen and his arm was all bandaged.

'You broke my nose and smashed up my Ferrari,' he said.

'I'm sorry,' I replied.

He looked at me for a moment, then punched me in the face. I heard a noise like a nut being cracked, and the pain made my stomach heave.

'For the nose,' he said. 'We're quits.'

He went and sat down in the empty armchair. The other man stood up. He had greying hair.

'Do you know who he is?' he said, pointing to the man from the Ferrari.

I shook my head.

'Do you know who *I* am?'

I saw the scar going all the way across his face.

And I realised we were fucked.

'Who is he?' Panzarotto asked.

'Shut up, Panzarò, it's best if you shut up.'

'Good,' the man with the scar said. 'You're a bright kid.'

'I didn't know it belonged to you people,' I said.

The man with the scar nodded. 'So,' he said, 'how are we going to solve this problem?'

'However you want,' I said. 'You give the orders, we'll do anything you like.'

The man with the scar thought this over for a bit.

He came closer. He lit a cigarette and blew the smoke in my face.

'There may be a solution,' he said.

'Whatever you say, it's done,' I said.

'If you have the balls,' he said.

'Anything,' I said.

He nodded again.

'There's someone who's been disrespectful and needs seeing to.'

'All right,' I said.

'Think you can do it?' he asked.

'It's not that hard,' I said.

'Good.'

He lifted two fingers as a signal and one of the men in jackets came closer. The man with the scar opened his hand and the other man gave him a gun.

'But first,' he said, 'you have to give me a demonstration.'

'What do I have to do?' I asked.

He put the gun in my hand, then threw his cigarette on the floor and crushed it with his boot.

'You have to shoot someone,' he said.

He pointed to Panzarotto.

'What?'

'Kill him. Do that, and you can go home.'

I felt like I'd been given an electric shock and my head went back. First my head and then my shoulders. And a shiver went all down my spine.

'And if I don't?'

'I shoot you, and *he* goes home,' he said.

The acid from the beer came all the way up from my stomach into my mouth. But I forced myself to swallow. I couldn't think.

'Well?' he said. 'What's it to be?'

I tried to get a grip on the gun, but it was like my hand was dead, and I couldn't hold it properly. I tried to stand up, but my legs didn't seem to want to obey me. I tried two or three times and finally got to my feet.

Panzarotto was moaning, like some birds do at night. He seemed to be shivering all over. He wanted to say something but couldn't. From time to time, he bit on his dog tag and shook his head and moaned.

I gripped the gun tighter. It weighed a ton. I looked at the man with the scar. He had his hands in his pockets and was looking at me without moving. I turned to Panzarotto again, trying not to look him in the face.

'Ray-Ban,' he said. 'Ray-Ban, what are you going to do?'

Sweat was pouring off me. My heart was beating like a pneumatic drill. I couldn't breathe. A single step seemed to take an hour. Everything was spinning around me. I heard Panzarotto's voice repeating, 'Ray-Ban . . . Ray-Ban . . .'

Nothing else.

'Ray-Ban . . . Ray-Ban . . .'

I looked at him for a moment.

He was crying now. He'd peed in his trousers. I didn't think I had the bottle, I didn't think I could do it, and I started crying too.

But it was him or me – there was no other way out.

I looked at him and it was like he was gradually turning into an animal, like one of those dogs that's dying, with its stomach ripped out, but can't make up its mind to die. The pain passed and the only thing I felt was a kind of disgust. My heart started beating slower and my breathing went back to normal. I raised the gun.

'Ray-Ban . . .' he said again.

'It's over now, Panzarò,' I said. 'It's all over.'

Andrej Longo was born in Ischia and named in homage to Tolstoy's *War and Peace*. He has published several critically acclaimed short story collections and featured in many anthologies. *Ten* was longlisted for the Bagutta prize, the Piero Chiara prize and the Premio Nazionale di Narrativa Bergamo. When he isn't writing for theatre, radio or cinema, Andrej Longo works as a pizza-maker in Naples.

Howard Curtis has translated more than seventy books from Italian, French and Spanish. He has won the John Florio Prize, the Premio Campiello Europa and the Marsh Award for Children's Literature in Translation, and has twice been nominated for The *Independent* Foreign Fiction Prize.